My Werewolf Professor

EMILIA ROSE

Cover by: Covers by Christian

Editing by Heart Full of Reads

Proofreading by: Jovana Shirley, Unforeseen Editing

Emilia Rose

emiliarosewriting@gmail.com

Chapter One

CALLUM

Another semester. Another group of students who weren't interested in learning.

It was like this every year, but I still taught because the stories of the gods were still very much needed in today's society. The students who actually cared about it learned more about themselves than anyone I had met.

"Alpha Lee," Levi, one of my pack members, said from my university office door.

I glanced up from my desk, gathered the rest of the materials for the first day of Classics I taught to first- and second-year students, and nodded to the door to signal for him to enter. Levi shuffled into the room and closed it behind him, bowing his head.

While many of the students at Arcane University in New Hampshire knew about the paranormal that haunted these woods, some—even professors—were still human. If any one of them found out about us, The Wolf Council would chew me out.

"What is it?" I asked.

Levi stuffed his hands into his ripped jeans. "I spotted wolves from the Goldtooth Pack at our borders."

My entire body stiffened. "Goldtooth Pack? Are you sure?"

"Yes. Beta Milo told me to relay the information to you."

I drew my tongue across my teeth, feeling the prick of my canines. "Don't engage. If the Goldtooth Pack is here, they're looking for something and will do anything to find it, which includes killing our pack members."

Levi nodded and stepped toward the cherry oak door. "Will do," he said. And just as he was about to step out the door, I called his name. He paused in the hallway, tensing when a human professor walked opposite of him. "Yeah?"

"Go to class. I'll handle it," I ordered.

"But—"

"You're not missing another one of my classes. You're taking Classics again because you failed the first time."

"Can't you pass me? We—"

"No."

After rubbing his hand across his face and grumbling under his breath, he walked down the hall toward the auditorium, where class started in fifteen minutes. I hiked my bag over my shoulder, locked my office door behind me, and started toward the exit. I didn't have time to run back to my pack before class started; I had to get one of the patrols in the forest to do it.

Glancing down at my watch, I shoved the door open, the crisp fall air blowing through the scruff on my face. Someone stumbled back, a phone and some Classics books tumbling to the ground in the middle of the doorway.

She gasped and leaned down to grab them. "Oh my gosh. I'm so sorry!"

My breath caught in the back of my throat as her sweet scent drifted through the air.

Mate.

I crouched down and grabbed some of her books from the walkway, admiring the way strands of her dirty-blonde hair blew into her face. "It's my fault," I said, wanting to hear her voice again and so desperately wanting her to look at me.

In a moment, she glanced up at me with piercing blue-violet eyes. Cheeks flushing a rosy red, she grabbed her books from my hand, our fingers grazing against each other's. My wolf growled inside of me, demanding that he feel her skin against his again.

Mate.

"No, I was, uh, trying to find my class and not paying attention." She stood up and brushed out her knee-length black skirt that had a slight split in it, and my wolf went wild. "Is this the Classics Building?"

"It is."

In an attempt to control my wolf, I stuffed my hands into my pockets and clenched my fists.

She was a student who didn't know the campus; it was probably her first year. Touching her was forbidden, no matter how much I wanted her right here and right now. If The Wolf Council found out about it, they'd remove me and all the other teachers who were wolves from this place.

"Okay, thank you." She scooted by me and into the building. "I don't want to be late."

Forcing myself not to turn around to grab her by the waist and pull her closer, stuff my nose into the crook of her neck and breathe her in, I inhaled her scent until it disappeared completely. I hurried toward the forest, finding the first damn wolf I came across, and told him to relay the information back to my beta.

If our mind links worked for long distances, I would've done it myself.

But they didn't anymore, thanks to The Wolf Council.

After racing back to the building, I took a shortcut toward the auditorium, knowing that the only classics class in this building today was mine, which meant one thing—my mate would be there, sitting in one of the many desks and staring up at me with those breathtaking eyes almost every day for the rest of the semester.

Stepping into the class, I scanned the room for her, yet I couldn't pick up her scent from the hundred mixed smells of the students. I relaxed only slightly and walked down the auditorium steps to the front, giving everyone a tight smile when they looked up at me and began quieting down.

I placed my bag on the front desk and looked around the room again. The door opened, her scent drifting into the room and her clumsy, cute ass nearly tripping over the carpet as she walked into the room.

She tucked some dirty-blonde hair behind her ear, gnawed on her pretty pink bottom lip, and anxiously searched the small auditorium for a seat, brows furrowed together. I stiffened and stared at her, my heart thrashing against my chest.

Mate.

Canines lengthening, I pressed my lips together and let them cut into my gums because not everyone who attended Arcane University was a werewolf, including her. I didn't want to scare her out of my class just yet. I didn't even know her name.

When she looked at me, I sucked in a breath and quickly looked away. She slowly walked down the wooden stairs of the auditorium to the second row, glanced down the aisle to see if she could find a seat. There was one, right in the center, right where I could see her, look at her, watch her without it seeming creepy.

Instead, she moved even closer to the front row and sat down toward my right. I inhaled her sweet beachy scent. She smelled so good—too good. I wanted to sink my teeth into her neck, right here and right now, not caring who it was in front of. I needed her to be mine.

So. Fucking. Badly.

After sitting, she placed her laptop and phone on her desk. She chewed on her bottom lip and tapped on the messages on her phone, staring down at messages from someone that she hadn't seemed to respond to yet. A moment passed, and she shook her head and shut the phone off, then looked back up at me.

Being taken off guard by those breath-fucking-taking eyes, I cleared my throat and looked down at my computer screen, shifting through the names on my attendance list to find hers. In a hundred-student class, I would never take attendance, but it couldn't hurt to try to spot her name.

Gracey Neal
Malak Ivo
Selin Flowers
Antonina Nichols
Bria Benton
Codey Spence
Malachy Herbert
Cain Wheeler

"Hey," Levi said to her, sitting beside her and holding out a hand. "I'm Levi."

My hands balled into fists behind the desk, and I pressed my lips together to suppress a growl. While I wanted to break them apart right then and there, I wanted so desperately to hear her voice, wanted her name, *needed* to have more of her.

"Bria," she said, cheeks flushing again.

She was blushing.

My mate was blushing because of someone other than me.

"Don't touch her," I scolded Levi through the mind link.

Before she could shake his hand, Levi pulled away. She widened her eyes and gave him a small, embarrassed smile, then turned back toward her computer. Levi glanced up at me, brows furrowed together, but I ignored him and cleared my throat, silencing the other students.

"Welcome to Classics: Ancient Mythologies. I'm Professor Lee. Let's get started."

Chapter Two

BRIA

Professor Lee talked so freaking fast.

I typed furiously on my keyboard, trying to keep up between getting all the notes down and desperately trying not to stare at him. Walking around the front of the class with his biceps bulging against his tight dress shirt, dark brown scruff, and those piercing hazel eyes that I couldn't look into without warmth spreading through my core, he was the epitome of any Greek god we were learning about this semester.

When I had chosen to attend Arcane University, it *wasn't* because of the hot professors, but that was definitely a plus. I wasn't complaining, but … I figured that I wouldn't retain much this semester even though I so desperately wanted to. Mythology was my favorite subject, like, ever.

"I'll see you tomorrow, bright and early," Professor Lee said, crossing his huge arms over his chest and looking oh-so fine. "Don't forget about the readings. Pages three through eighteen in your textbook."

After typing the last of my notes, I glanced up to see the rest of the students already either heading out the door or forming a line in front of Professor Lee to introduce themselves. My advisor told me that I should introduce myself to my teachers, but ... I was always so nervous around people.

I told her that I wasn't going to, but Professor Lee kept glancing over at me during class. Part of me wanted to go over to him to at least apologize for bumping into him earlier. I didn't know *what* possessed me to do something so out of character, but I found myself lingering at the very back of the line, letting people cut me to talk to him first because my stomach was in knots.

The last student said her good-byes to him, walked out of the auditorium, and left me there alone with him. Alone with a hell of a man who I couldn't stop gawking at.

He stared at me with a pair of hazel eyes and smiled. "Hi."

"Hi, I'm Bria."

I shifted from foot to foot, not knowing what to say. I didn't have *anything* planned to say. I didn't even have plans to come up here and introduce myself to him. If I did, I would've practiced in front of the mirror in my dorm room until I knew I didn't look so awkward and stupid.

"I wanted to, um ..."

He leaned against the front of his desk and thrust his hands into his pants pockets, full lips set in a small smile. "Bria," he said, my name rolling off his tongue so naturally that it did something to me that it really freaking shouldn't have.

Warmth gathered in my core, my heart racing a bit faster.

"Bria." I repeated my name like a dumbass, completely absorbed in how attractive my Classics professor was.

He had to be at least in his early forties, his dark scruff decorated with silver specs and a crease between his brows. And I was just an eighteen-year-old kid who went to college to run away from her family.

"Sorry," I said quickly, cheeks flushing. "I'm ... I, uh, wanted to say that I'm looking forward to Classics. I've been obsessed with mythology since I was, like, five, so I'm excited to read some more this semester." With his intense gaze on me, I looked down at my feet and scrambled to hike my backpack up my shoulder. "I should get—"

"Which is your favorite?" he asked quickly, kicking himself off the desk and moving a couple inches closer to me.

My breath caught in the back of my throat, my heart pounding in my chest.

"My favorite?" I asked almost in a whisper by how close he was.

"Favorite story, favorite god?"

"Oh, um, Hephaestus isn't my favorite god, but I've reread stories about him a couple times."

"Any particular reason?"

Cheeks flushed, I shifted from foot to foot and tried hard not to gaze up into his hazel eyes that seemed to look right through me. I sucked in a breath and found myself staring anyway, the tension between us growing by the moment. He was close, and I couldn't get myself to move away, and I didn't want to either.

"I don't know," I whispered.

He paused and arched a hard brown brow, lips curling into a smirk. "Well, you have all semester to figure it out. Everyone gravitates toward a story or a person for a reason." He lifted his finger, and I thought he was going to push a strand of hair behind my ear. But instead, he stopped midway and drew his fingers across the scruff on his face.

"What's your favorite story?" I asked.

After a moment, he paused and cracked another breathtaking smile. "You'll find out with time, Bria."

When he said my name, tingles rushed through me. "Anyway ..." I glanced down and tried hard to ignore them. "Sorry for bumping into you earlier. I'll be more careful tomorrow." I took a couple steps backward. "Bright and early."

"Bright and early," Professor Lee repeated.

After giving him one last smile, my cheeks flaming hot, I turned on my heel and hurried up the auditorium stairs, careful not to trip again. "Get yourself together, Bria," I whispered to myself once I started up the walkway toward the exit.

He was my Classics professor, for fuck's sake, and it was the first damn day of college.

It was forbidden.

Chapter Three

CALLUM

"Why are Goldtooth Pack wolves near our property?" I asked Milo, pacing on the cream tiled floors of my home office. Fingers running through my scruff, I tried fucking hard to think straight, but Bria seemed to be all I could think about.

Goldtooth wolves were some of the most ruthless around, originating about two hours south, near a beach town. They had killed two humans last year during tourist season, and those were only the ones the police found.

I was not about to have them come near *my* property, especially not when *my mate* was human and couldn't protect herself against fiends who would do anything to get some even if that meant raping and killing an innocent girl.

Milo sat on one of my two saffron couches, tapping his finger against the leather. "We've watched them all day and couldn't uncover the reason why they're here. Don't think we will be able to without engaging."

After pushing out a breath, I shook my head and headed for the door. "Don't engage unless they do first. You know what they're capable of. It's too risky for us to start anything with college back in session."

"Where are you going?" Milo asked.

"I need a run."

Once I grabbed a spare set of training clothes, I headed out on a needle-covered path back toward the university. I never ran on their trails, especially during school months, but my wolf had been aching to search for Bria again. It had barely been a couple hours.

"Find mate now."

I pushed myself harder, inhaling the calming scent of softwood. Leaves rustled gently above me, rays of sun slipping through the tree branches. When I found myself jogging onto Arcane University property, I slowed and decided on a trail that would take me throughout the campus, an easy way to pick up her scent.

Students sat on benches and at picnic tables, eating early dinners. Others passed a volleyball back and forth on the square. And then there was Bria, who lay on her stomach, reading her classics book for tomorrow, on the lawn in front of a dormitory.

Like a fucking creep, I stopped about fifty feet away from her and watched her flip page after page, smiling to herself like she was actually enjoying the reading. Nobody ever enjoyed classics books—at least not in the classes I taught. Strands of her dirty-blonde hair swept into her face, and it took everything inside of me not to walk over to her and tuck them behind her ear. Goddess, I had wanted to do that this morning too.

Rubbing a hand over my face, I shook my head and turned away. I couldn't fucking do this. Why the hell was I standing around and watching one of my students? If she saw me gawking at her, she could report me to the board and get me kicked out. Worse than that, The Wolf Council would find out about it too.

"I have an idea," my wolf said in my mind.

"What?" I asked, desperate for something to get me closer to her.

Before I could stop, I found myself heading right in her direction, my legs moving on their fucking own, thanks to my wolf.

"What are you doing?" I scolded.

"Going to talk to mate."

"That's your idea?!"

When he didn't respond, I dug my heels into the ground and forced myself to stop ten feet away. Ten fucking feet. And in the midst of the softwood and food from the café a street down, all I could focus on was her sweet beachy scent that did nothing but drive me fucking crazy for her.

"Professor Lee!" someone called to my left.

From the corner of my eye, I saw Bria look over at me. And being the alpha I was, I couldn't help but feel my body tense. Not because I was nervous she saw me staring at her, but because I wanted her to like *me*, to find *me* attractive in the sea of frat boys and horny college kids from Arcane University.

"Hi," I said, giving the girl a small smile.

Don't look over at Bria. Don't look over at Bria. Don't look over at Bria.

I glanced over at Bria, my gaze lingering for a moment longer than it should've. She gave me a soft, small smile, then looked back at her textbook. When she pushed her legs a bit closer together and I smelled her cunt, I nearly lost it.

"Do we have—" the girl started.

"A quiz tomorrow morning?" I finished, canines extending. "Yes. Don't forget to read."

It was a lie. I didn't have *any* quiz planned for tomorrow, but I guessed I had one now because I needed to get the fuck out of here before my wolf seized complete control of my body and took Bria on the university lawn.

All I could imagine was running my nose down her neck and sinking my canines into her neck, claiming her, taking her, making her mine. I'd bet her pussy tasted so fucking good. One damn smell of it, and my wolf had already gone wild.

Turning my back toward Bria, I gave the girl a forced smile and jogged in the opposite direction, passing Levi and only stopping when I stepped into the forest. I rested my back against a tree, taking deep breaths to suppress my wolf.

"Hey!" Levi called with a grin, jogging in Bria's direction. "Bria, right?"

I tensed and glanced from behind the tree to see them chatting. My hands balled into fists, anger rushing through me so heavily that even with my enhanced hearing as a wolf, I couldn't seem to listen. All I saw was him making my mate smile *again.*

After a moment, Levi nodded and turned back to the forest.

When he reached me, I growled, forcing him to stop right in his damn fucking tracks. "Don't touch Bria."

"I was just inviting her to a party. She's a first-year and—"

Unable to stop myself, I wrapped my hand around the front of his throat and thrust him against a tree, my canines lengthening past my lips and my claws nearly cutting into his neck. "Don't fucking touch her. Do you understand me?"

Levi widened his eyes at me. "Yes."

"Yes?"

"Yes, Alpha," he said, bowing his head.

I shoved him away from me and looked back at Bria, who now lay on her back and shielded her eyes from the setting sun as she continued reading her classics book. I should claim her right here, right now. No horny fraternity asshole should have his hands all over my mate at a party.

Bria Benton was mine. Only mine.

Chapter Four

BRIA

After pulling on my fifth outfit for the night, I stood in front of the mirror and sighed at my reflection. Love handles, love handles, and more freaking love handles. All of my party clothes were either too tight around the waist that it shoved all my fat above the beltline or fit me perfectly but didn't look sexy.

There was no way that I was going to my first frat party ever, looking like *this*.

So, I changed out my jeans for sweatpants and my halter top for the tank top that I slept in for the past four nights, then threw my hair into a messy bun—and by messy, I didn't mean cute like all those girls on social media. I meant, hair-sticking-up-in-every-direction messy.

Typing on her phone, Jasmine opened our dorm room door and glanced up at me. "Why aren't you ready?"

I gnawed on the inside of my cheek. "I'm not going."

"Come on, Bria. It's our first semester of college. Don't you want to have some fun?"

"Yeah, but I don't have anything to wear."

"You can wear something of mine."

Cutting my gaze to her, I raised a brow. She and I both knew that I would never fit into anything her petite ass could. I'd pop all the buttons on her shirt and stretch out her leggings until they became sweatpants on her. So, that was a no from me.

She rolled her eyes. "You'll look great in anything that you have."

"Everyone at this school is insanely small and skinny, Jasmine. It's like everyone takes three-hour runs every day to stay fit. I don't want to go like this."

I shook my head and scrolled through my emails, finding one from Professor Lee, addressed to the entire class.

Class,

There will be a five-question quiz on tonight's reading. Be prepared. If you have any questions, feel free to email me back. I'll get back to you as soon as I can.

Sincerely,

Professor Lee

"Nobody cares what you look like at frat parties," Jasmine said. "Half the guys are drunk off their asses anyway. They see a cute face like yours, and they'll be all over you. Don't worry too much about it, Bria. Let's just go."

I grabbed my classics book from my desk. "I'll come next time. I have a quiz tomorrow."

"What?! Who's the psycho who assigned a quiz on the first day of school?"

"Professor Lee."

"You have Professor Lee?" she asked with wide eyes. "Isn't he the most gorgeous person that you've ever seen?"

"Do you have him?" I asked, curious as to how she found out about him already. She was a first-year student like me and wasn't taking any classics classes as far as I knew. She must've been on RateMyProfessor.com or something.

She paused, opening and closing her mouth, then hurried to the door. “Oh, I ... saw him in the hallway. One of my friends has his class. Anyway, have fun studying. Next time, you’re coming out with me. See ya.”

When she closed the door, I slumped my shoulders forward and let out a breath. That was ... easier than I thought it would be. At first, she was so adamant about me going with her, and then she quickly dropped it.

Deciding not to think so much about it, I sat at my desk, opened my book, and studied for the next five hours until twelve a.m.. Jasmine still wasn’t home yet, and even though she told me that she wouldn’t be home until after two a.m., I was still worried. Was that what people did in college? Stay up until all hours of the night?

As I closed my textbook and hopped up onto the bed, my phone lit up with an email notification.

Bria,

Have you read this?

https://www.amazon.com/ahd ...

—Callum Lee

I gnawed on the inside of my cheek and suppressed a smile, my cheeks flushing for no good reason at all. Professor Lee didn’t sign his professional name like he did when he sent an email to the entire class earlier, but he signed his real name to me.

Callum Lee.

And an email after midnight?

Callum—Professor Lee was up late, thinking about me.

Surely, it didn’t mean anything, but the thought of my hot professor thinking about me and our conversation this late at night did something *bad* to me. I pressed my thighs together, like I did while watching him run around the campus until he stopped and saw me gawking at him earlier. God, he looked so sexy with a layer of sweat covering his body and his muscles swelling underneath his shirt.

I swallowed hard and clicked on the link, getting directed to a book titled *The Red Hammer*, which explored the tales of Hephaestus and his relationship with his mother.

While I thought I read everything on that god—at least within the classics books—I hadn't touched this one yet. I made a mental note to pick it up tomorrow in the school library and typed out a quick reply back to Professor Lee, unable to stop myself.

Professor Lee,

It's added to my TBR list! Thanks for the recommendation.

Sincerely,

Bria

After scrunching my nose, I erased my sign-off, then typed the same exact words over again. I couldn't decide if it was too formal or not formal enough. But he wasn't formal at all in his email. Deciding not to overthink it, I hit Send and placed my phone facedown on my stomach, smiling stupidly to myself as I stared up at the ceiling.

Here I was, a first-year college student, who declined attending a frat party in order to lie in her bed and get butterflies that her much older professor was emailing her this late at night. It was a damn fantasy that would *never* come true, a small act of good attention that I ached for.

It wasn't like I ever got that at home.

Shutting off my bedside lamp, I closed my eyes and felt the phone vibrate against my stomach. I tilted the phone up slightly, so the brightness wouldn't blind me, and shot up in the bed when I saw another email from Professor Lee.

I think you'll enjoy it. It's one of my favorites.

—Callum

No *Callum Lee* this time. Just Callum.

My stomach fluttered. I hugged the phone to my chest and smiled like a complete idiot at the ceiling, then shook my head and plugged my phone into the charger. I couldn't be stupid. I was making something out of nothing, and if I didn't control myself, that something was going to control me.

Tomorrow, I'd thank Professor Lee for the recommendation

again and get the book from the library. That would be it; I'd be done with the little crush I formed because I needed to study this semester. I had worked damn hard to find the money to attend college without the help from Mom or Dad. I couldn't let it go to waste.

Chapter Five

CALLUM

"As promised"—I passed out sheets of paper with quiz questions on the front—"a five-question quiz about the assigned reading last night. For those of you who recently switched into my class, this quiz will have to be made up during office hours."

After a collective groan, the room became quiet, everyone taking out pens or pencils to complete the quiz as quickly as they could so they could leave. Bria answered the questions at lightning speed, like she was ready for it, and it made me smile. In all my years of teaching, I hadn't found anyone as enthusiastic about this material as I was. But now … my mate was here.

"When you're finished, please drop your quizzes up front."

Once everyone began finishing up, Bria sat at her desk in the front row. From where I stood, I could tell that she had answered all the questions and even written an explanation for one. But she still didn't get up. It was as if she was waiting for everyone else to leave first.

And when Levi, the last person to finish, stood, she did too.

"Bria …" Levi swung his backpack over his shoulder and smiled.

My blood fucking boiled. This kid didn't listen to a word I fucking said yesterday.

"Enjoy your night in? Jasmine said you wanted to study instead of party. Kinda makes you seem like a *lo-ser*, if you ask me."

"Well, if you ask *me*, nobody cool sounds out the word *loser* anymore," Bria said, gathering her notebooks and returning Levi's smirk. "But I had a great time, thank you. I got some studying in and"—she glanced in my direction, looking right fucking at me watching her, blushed, then looked away—"I found my next good read."

"Who reads anymore? I don't."

"And that's why you failed my class last semester, Levi," I interrupted, loathing the fucking way he stood so close to her. I wanted to rip her away, claim her. It hadn't even been two days yet, and she was already driving me wild.

Bria smiled and raised her brows at Levi. "Maybe you should be doing that instead of partying on a Monday night."

Levi shook his head, turned to me, and handed me his paper. "You know, I aced the quiz. One hundred percent. Check it out."

I glossed over the answers and raised my brows. "This is good, Levi. You're off to a better start this year." I gave him my best professor smile and continued the conversation through our mind link. *"But if you don't stop messing with Bria Benton, you won't be."*

Straightening his back, Levi gave us a tense smile and waved us off. "Well, I gotta get going. Don't want to be late. See ya." And with that, he was off, rushing up the aisle and out of the room.

After Levi exited the room, leaving Bria and me alone again, she hiked her backpack onto her shoulder and handed me her quiz. "Here you go. I was stuck between two answers for question four, so I wrote a detailed description as to why I thought it was the answer I chose."

I took the quiz from her, my fingers brushing against her slender ones, and my wolf howled inside of me. The mere touch sent tingles up and down my arms, her scent becoming even more powerful somehow.

"Mate. Claim mate."

After I glanced over her answers, a warmth spread throughout my chest. "Oh, Bria, you've gotten everything right, except ..."

"Except?" she asked with big eyes, staring down at the quiz and going over the questions and answers again. She looked to be one of those students who stayed up all hours of the night, studying for a simple five-question quiz, needing to get all the answers correct. "It's question four, isn't it?"

"Your name."

She placed a hand over her heart and let out a breath, staring down at the empty line on the top of the sheet for her name. "Oh gosh ..."

"You could get points taken off for such a simple mistake."

"I wouldn't be able to ... to make those points up somehow?"

My breath caught in the back of my throat, and I didn't know if Bria really wanted extra credit or if she was flirting. All I knew was that my wolf was going wild for her right now. I needed more, a taste, something to calm him.

"For you, Bria, there will be extra credit, but I don't think you'll be needing it."

Though I hoped she would.

"What if I wanted it?" She gnawed on the inside of her cheek, then quickly followed up with, "You know, in case I fail a quiz or an exam or ... *something else.* I just ... I want to make sure that it's an option for me."

Unable to stop myself, I grasped her chin and forced her to look me in the eye. "It will always be an option for you. I'll have extra credit for whenever you need it. Discipline too."

"Discipline," Bria whispered, shuffling her feet. "So, I, um ..." She hugged the book to her chest and lingered at her desk. "I saw you running yesterday afternoon. Do you run every day around the quad?"

"I do." *Lie.*

I *never* ran around the quad, but I did now. If Bria studied on the grass every afternoon like she had yesterday, I'd be running around this campus every day to see her. It was that or stalk her dorm room, which would definitely get me kicked out by the council.

She became quiet, her thighs suddenly pressing together. "Good to know."

"You're welcome to come with me sometime."

Fuck, why did I fucking say that? She's my student, for Goddess's sake.

Instead of taking it back—because she wasn't only my student, but she was my mate too—I leaned against the desk and patiently waited for her answer, my wolf growing restless inside of me every time she blushed.

"God, no," Bria said, eyes widening in surprise. She glanced up at me through her lashes. "I mean, it's not that I don't want to. I would love to run with you. I ..." Her cheeks turned even redder, as if she thought she was digging herself an even bigger grave. But I couldn't get enough of it. Eventually, she looked back down at her shoes. "I just hate running. Kinda with a passion."

"Hate running?" I asked, crossing my arms. "What do you do for exercise?"

To my surprise, Bria looked me right in the eye with her cheeks still flushing and said, "Other things." Her voice was filled with a tinge of sultriness, and I couldn't stop myself from thinking about bending her right over my lap and punishing her for making me so fucking hard during class today.

I inhaled the sweet scent of her salivating cunt.

Goddess, Bria was going to fucking destroy me. One of these days, I wouldn't be able to handle myself. I'd throw my office door open, pull her into the room, and claim her with everything I had, my teeth in her neck, my tongue on her pussy, my hands all over her body.

After a few moments of silence, she smiled and pulled away.

"Anyway, I should get going. I need to get to the library to pick up that book you suggested before my next class. I'll see you tomorrow."

"Don't let mate leave."

"Wait," I said, stuffing my hand into my bag, pulling out *The Red Hammer*, and handing it to her. "I had this copy lying around back home. Take it."

She stared at it with wide eyes. "Are you sure? I don't want to take your personal copy."

"It's fine. Just return it when you're finished." I collected the messed up stack of quizzes on my desk. "I hope you enjoy it."

Chapter Six

BRIA

"How was Lee's class?" Jasmine asked, lying on her stomach on the quad and staring at her phone, her unopened books in a pile beside her. She glanced up for a brief moment and wiggled her eyebrows. "Isn't he, like, a *god*?"

My lips curled into a small smile, and I turned the page of my book. Since I left class this morning, I hadn't been able to put it down. It was about three hundred pages and forty sections long, but it was so good that I hadn't done any of my actual homework yet.

And I might've wanted Professor Lee to see me with it.

Earlier in class ... gosh, I didn't know what got into me when I asked him about that extra credit. Both of us knew extra credit wasn't what I was asking about, and he seemed to go along and even enjoyed the way I was speaking to him.

I shook my head, letting my hair blow into my face. Maybe I wasn't forward enough. Maybe he really was looking out for his students. And maybe I was just looking way too much into this entire thing.

"Earth to Bria!" Jasmine said. "Daydreaming about *Callum Lee*?"

"Definitely not."

She playfully rolled her eyes and kicked her legs back and forth. "I'm thinking about switching into his class. I mean, if *you're* not going to hit on him, then someone has to, right? Can't let a man who looks like *that* slip through your fingers."

My hands tightened around the book until my fingers turned white. A burst of anger suddenly rushed through me, or maybe it was jealousy because Jasmine was a thousand and one times prettier and skinnier than I was. If she switched into our class, then Professor Lee wouldn't pay a single ounce of attention to me.

And I wanted all of his attention.

I had never gotten any before.

"Yeah," I lied, heart pounding. "That would be cool."

Fuck.

After turning the page harshly, I looked up at the right time to see Professor Lee on his daily run around the quad. Shirtless, dripping in sweat, and muscles flexed so hard that I could see the veins in his biceps, he took the same path that he had yesterday.

"There he is!" Jasmine squealed.

Instead of listening to her talk about her obsession with him—I was far too angry and too ... horny after his class to deal with it—I slapped my book shut and gathered my belongings, standing up before he could run over here. "I gotta go. I have class. See you tonight."

Before she could respond, I hurried toward the classics building and slipped through the doors, but not before glancing over my shoulder at Professor Lee one last time, feeling the warmth between my legs.

Once inside, I searched for a bathroom. After class, I had gone all day without a release, all day haunted by those piercing hazel eyes, so I needed something now. And I didn't want to work myself up over Jasmine transferring into our class.

Just as I was about to slip into the women's restroom, I caught sight of an office door cracked open a smidgen and the name *Professor Lee* written beside it. I stopped in my tracks, heart pounding, and inched closer to it.

Professor Lee must've been gone for a quick run, if he left his door open.

I should ... go.

Yet I found myself opening the door and peering into the room. Before I knew it, I stepped into his office and closed the door behind me, breathing in his sultry scent that did nothing but drive me mad with lust.

I dropped my books right to the ground.

I didn't know what I was doing, what had come over me.

But I couldn't stop myself from walking over to his desk and putting my scent on everything that he owned. Part of me wanted him to know that I was here; the other part knew that he wouldn't be able to pick up my scent in a room as large as this. There must've been hundreds of people a week that came in and out of here, and I'd just be another one of his students.

Still, that didn't stop me from thinking about how sexy he looked during his run today.

It wasn't muscle like a bodybuilder with every fiber bulging through the skin, but muscle of a mountain man who chopped wood with an ax for hours a day. But Callum Lee was no mountain man; he was a professor. My fucking professor who I was now about to shamelessly masturbate to.

Thick muscle glistening with a layer of sweat. Dark hazel sinister eyes. Fingers so big, thick, callous. If he grabbed me by the throat, shoved me to my knees, and told me to suck him off, I would without any questions asked.

I leaned back on the desk, shoved two fingers into my panties, and rubbed them fast against my clit, a whimper escaping my lips. I shouldn't be here, but ... but I didn't want to leave. I couldn't go back out on the quad and face Jasmine again while my pussy pulsed, thinking about that man.

No, I wanted to come.

In his office.

On his desk.

All over his papers.

Collapsing into his chair, I kicked one foot up on his desk to spread my legs and rubbed my clit harder and faster, the pressure rising in my core. If he caught me here, doing this, I could be dismissed from college. I would have to find my own way or go back home to Mom and Dad. And yet, somehow, I couldn't seem to give a single fuck about that now. Not after the way he stared at me during class this morning.

I squeezed my eyes closed and imagined Professor Lee stuffing his face between my legs, his dark scruff tickling my thighs and decorated with my juices, his thick fingers plunging into my tight pussy.

"Oh my gosh," I whispered, toes curling in my sandals.

The pressure rose in my core, my entire body tensing. I pressed my legs together and slapped a hand over my mouth to scream into it as wave after wave of pleasure coursed through my body. Everything about this felt too good, and I knew even after I walked out of his office—hopefully undetected—I would scurry back to my room, shove my hand into my panties, and touch myself while thinking about Professor Lee again tonight.

Chapter Seven

CALLUM

Before I went for my run, I saw Bria sitting on the lawn in front of the classics building. It was almost as if she was waiting for me to come out and see her. At least, that was what I wanted to believe, but I couldn't quite figure her out yet. I didn't know if this attraction was mutual yet.

But when I finally made it out into the sun, she wasn't anywhere to be found. Jasmine sat in her spot, grinning at me like she always had since she turned eighteen a few months ago. I didn't know where she scared Bria off to, but I couldn't stop myself from finding out.

"Hi, Alpha," Jasmine said, rolling onto her back and leaning back on her forearms when I approached her.

I growled low. "It's Professor Lee here, Jasmine. You know that."

She bowed her head. "Sorry, Professor Lee. What're you doing out here? Levi said that you never run around the campus."

Instead of entertaining her, I cut to the chase, my wolf needing to find Bria, needing to smell her, needing to take her now. Her scent lingered so heavily in the air here, and I couldn't stop thinking about how her cunt smelled during class today when she kept pressing her thighs together.

"Where's Bria?"

"Bria?" she asked, brows furrowed. "Why do you want—"

"Where. Is. She?"

Jasmine widened her eyes and pointed toward the classics building. "She said that she had class. She headed toward the classics building." She paused. "I didn't think she had any classics classes besides yours, but—"

Without listening to another word she said—I couldn't help it—I hurried toward the classics building. Bria didn't have any other classes in this building. I was sure of it. I might have ... checked in one of the school's computers late last night. That didn't matter though. What mattered was that Bria only came to this building for me ... and I wasn't in my office.

Stepping into the building, I followed her scent from the main hallway to a side hallway near my office. And as I walked into the corridor, she rushed out of my office. She shut the door behind her and stopped when she looked up and saw me standing at the end of the hall.

Eyes widening, cheeks flushing, she parted her lips to say something, but the only words to come out of her mouth were, "Professor Lee," in nothing but a raspy whisper.

I inhaled sharply and found my shorts tightening at the thick, sweet scent drifting down the hallway from her. "What are you doing here?" I asked rougher than I meant to, but my wolf was quickly clawing his way to the surface, ready to come out and bite her already.

She held her books to her chest and walked slowly down the hallway toward me, eyeing the exit door to my right. "I was, um, looking for you. I wanted to ask you something about this, um, book."

My teeth lengthened into canines inside my mouth, my nails into claws behind my back. That scent was coming from her cunt, her sopping, salivating cunt that I wanted to bury my face in and eat until she was crying out for me. If I didn't get out of here soon, I'd do it too.

"But I have class now." Bria hurried toward the door, gaze focused on the ground. "I don't want to be late."

Before she could pass me, I posted my hand on the wall beside me to block her exit. "Come back after your class. I expect to see you during my office hours. You don't have class during them."

After giving me a curt nod, she hurried down the hallway without looking me in the eye, and I let her. Once Bria left the classics building, I hurried into my office and slammed and locked the door, the scent of her arousal hitting me in waves.

I rushed to my desk, and when I saw a wet spot on my chair that smelled like Bria's cunt, I growled. I couldn't stop myself from collapsing in that same chair, shoving my hand into my running shorts, and pulling my cock out. After spitting on my hand, I stroked my cock, getting harder and harder by the damn second at the thought of my mate wanting me to take her so fucking bad that she locked herself into my office while I was running and touched herself.

"Oh, Bria, you're going to get me in so much trouble," I murmured to myself.

I moved my hand up and down my dick, tightening it more by the moment, picturing her cheeks all flushed as she stuffed two fingers inside her tight cunt and finger-fucked herself until her pussy was drooling all over my office furniture.

Growling, I moved my hips up and down, imagining pounding myself into Bria, grasping her ass, and watching her pale cheeks turn pink. After closing my eyes, I pictured the night I would finally get to plunge my teeth into her and take her completely, biting her neck, licking up her blood, making myself part of her.

"Fuck," I drew out, stroking my cock up and down, hard and fast.

I inhaled sharply, taking in as much of her scent as I could, and came into my hand. I didn't care what I thought or what the council would do to me for having a relationship with one of my students. Bria wanted this as much as I did.

Chapter Eight

BRIA

Two hours later, I stood at Professor Lee's office door with my stomach in knots and *The Red Hammer* pulled tight to my chest. Earlier, I had lied to Professor Lee. I didn't have class; I went straight back to my dorm room, showered, shaved, and maybe ... thought about what kind of damn excuse I could give him for sitting in his office with the door closed.

I didn't think he believed that I was only there to talk.

That was what office hours were for, and for some ungodly reason, I decided to show up to his hours about two minutes before they were about to end now. I told myself that maybe I didn't know what to say to him and wanted it to be a quick and sweet meeting.

But the reason I was here right before Callum Lee ended his dedicated hours was because I didn't want him to be paying attention to anyone else while I was here. I wanted his attention. I wanted him more than I should admit.

Deciding that I'd never come up with an excuse, I stepped into his office. A girl from my class sat at his desk with her brows furrowed together and our class textbook in front of her. Lee stood behind her with one large hand posted on his desk and the other pointing to a piece of text on the page.

When I stepped into the room, Professor Lee immediately looked up and sucked in a breath, hazel eyes flickering gold for a moment. I gave him a tight smile, not knowing what else to do, and lingered by his desk, not liking how close he was to her.

It wasn't even anything sexual or anything flirtatious, just a professor helping his student, but, God, it made me angrier than it should've. I didn't know what came over me; I'd never felt this way for someone, even in high school.

The girl glanced over her shoulder, then up at Professor Lee. It looked like they shared some kind of look or hidden message or something because the girl stood up and hurried out of the room.

"Bria." Professor Lee cleared his throat and moved around his desk to his chair, sitting. "Close the door."

My breath caught in my throat, and I shut the door after the student left in a hurry. With my back turned toward him, I told myself that this didn't mean anything, that I was here to talk to him about *The Red Hammer*, that a freshman girl who loved classics didn't mean anything to him, and that I shouldn't get my hopes up.

Once I finally gathered enough courage to turn back toward him, I sat in the seat across from him and crossed my legs to suppress my aching cunt. My mind wandered back to Jasmine, who casually mentioned that if I didn't flirt with Professor Lee, then she would. And I didn't want to picture Lee between anyone else's thighs, except mine.

Though I could never go through with something like that. Blatantly and openly flirting with a professor and asking him to eat me out, to fuck me even ... those things only happened in porn and never to the shy girl who got nervous every time she had to talk to her professor. Jasmine *was* the type to bang the professor. Not me.

"I didn't think you'd show up," Lee said, pulling me out of my thoughts.

"Sorry if I'm late. I know that your office hours are finished right about now."

"I have all night," Professor Lee said quickly.

"I wanted to return this book to you." I handed the book back to him, the same one he had given me this morning.

Lee took the book from my hands, brows furrowed together. "You don't want to read it?"

"I've already finished."

He stared at me with wide hazel eyes. "It's only been a couple hours, and it's almost a three-hundred-page book. You finished it?"

"Yes," I said, finally relaxing under his intense gaze. "I really enjoyed it."

For the next three hours, we chatted about *The Red Hammer*, the characters, what they meant to classics scholars, what they meant to him, and finally ... what they meant to me, which was by far the hardest thing that I'd ever had to talk about. All the scholars analyzed the way that Hera hated her son Hephaestus until she wanted something from him, but an analysis wasn't what I got from the book.

It was the heartbreak Hephaestus went through every day, the pain, the agony of not fitting in, of being hated by everyone who was supposed to love you. Those were things an analysis from a bunch of scholars could never tell you, could never make you feel unless you went through it every day.

"Your parents ..." Lee trailed off after I gave my opinion on the book.

"Are assholes," I finished, glancing down at my lap and not wanting to talk much more about it. I hated talking about them, hated thinking about them, hated being around them. Every time I thought back to being home with them again, I wanted to disappear forever.

After a couple of silent, awkward moments, I realized that I told him way more than I should've. He was my classics professor, not a therapist and not someone who cared about *me.* I pulled out my phone.

The screen read six forty-five p.m., and I widened my eyes. I didn't want to leave, but … I didn't want to keep him much longer. He probably had to get home to a girlfriend or … a family or someone way more important than me. The mere thought made my heart clench.

"I should probably go. I don't want to keep you."

Just as I was about to stand, Professor Lee grabbed my wrist. "Stay. I don't have anyone else to see tonight. I cleared my schedule out for you." He pulled his phone out of his desk drawer. "And I had a pizza for us scheduled for seven."

Eyes even wider, I stared at him with my breath caught in the back of my throat and heat growing between my legs. "For me?" I asked, voice barely above a whisper. My heart pounded inside my chest, pussy clenching.

Professor Lee paused. "Unless you have something else to do tonight."

"No." I relaxed back against the chair again and pressed my thighs together harder. "Just you." Realizing what I had said, I slapped a hand over my mouth, my cheeks burning. "I didn't mean it like that. I, uh …"

"Sure you didn't," Professor Lee said.

Cursing quietly to myself, I pressed my thighs harder together.

Professor Lee was flirting with me. *Me.*

And so I stayed a while longer, ate dinner with him, and moved to sit behind his desk with him as he showed me a couple other books that he thought I'd like, never once bringing up my family again.

At the end of the night, when I finally decided that I should definitely leave, we stood outside his office door, inches apart from each other.

I didn't want to leave, but it was so late, and night classes would be finished soon. Students would flood these halls in a few moments and see us together like this. And someone might think that this looked like more than what it was.

Still, I couldn't help lingering by his door and trying to find something else to talk to him about. He was closer than I expected him to be, his intense gaze focused on me and pulling me in. The heat grew between my legs, and I shifted from foot to foot, knowing that I would touch myself later, thinking about tonight.

"What's wrong?" he finally said, glancing down to my thighs and inhaling sharply.

"Nothing," I breathed out. "I'm just ... so uncomfortable."

There were a few moments of silence between us, and then he said, "What if I ate your cunt?"

Heat rushed to my core. "Wh-what?"

He swallowed, hazel eyes widening slightly. "Did I just—"

"Yes," I said before he could finish, my pussy throbbing at the mere thought of Professor Lee between my legs, hungrily eating my pussy until I became a sopping mess of juices on his office desk. Unable to stop myself, I grabbed his hand and pressed my back to his large wooden office door. "Please."

Reaching behind me, I wiggled his doorknob and pushed the door open to slip into the room with him for a second time tonight. My heart was racing, my breath catching. A brief moment went by when I thought I misheard him.

But then something flashed in his eyes, a tint of gold, of hunger, of lust.

With his heel, he kicked the door closed, wrapped his strong hands around my waist, set me on his desk, and yanked my panties to my knees. "Fuck, Bria, I've been waiting to taste you for days now."

Before I could stop him, he spread my legs apart and buried his face between my thighs, his scruff tickling my folds. He inhaled sharply, a low rumble coming from his chest, and then pressed his soft lips against my clit.

"Professor," I said in a breath.

We were really doing this with students right in the hall.

"The door ... it's ... so thin." I could hear everyone roaming around outside.

"Then, you'd better keep quiet, Bria," he murmured against me, fingers pulling my folds apart. When he had better access to my clit, he flicked his tongue against the sensitive skin and sent a wave of pleasure throughout my entire body.

And after the first taste, he lost complete control, savagely sucking and licking and burying his face deep between my legs. My juices decorated his thick, dark scruff, his eyes flickering from hazel to gold.

He was like a hungry wolf.

Chapter Nine

CALLUM

Bria lay on my desk on the brink of an orgasm with her body tense and her eyes squeezed closed. I paused right before she came, feeling my wolf about to break free and gain control of me. And I knew that if I heard that pretty mouth saying my name while her legs trembled around my shoulders, fuck, I'd lose it.

I'd transform into my beast right here and right now in front of a human.

"More," Bria breathed out, her voice so raspy.

Hell, I wanted to make her scream my name so fucking bad that it hurt me to pull away.

"Bria, you have to leave," I said, staring down at the wooden floor between her legs. No matter how much I wanted to, I couldn't look up at her pleading eyes or listen to her breathy moans any longer. I was moments from shifting with all these fucking students outside and Bria here with me.

She leaned back on her forearms. "Is something wron—"

"Now, Bria. Get out." I quickly stood and turned my back to her, so she couldn't see the canines in my mouth or my golden eyes. If I scared her off now, she might not want to mate me, and if she didn't want to mate me, then my wolf would force himself on her.

I knew he'd do it too.

He had been waiting for her since we were eighteen, for twenty-five fucking years.

Bria jumped off the desk and pushed down her skirt. When she went to pull up her panties, I gripped them in my hand and ripped them right off her.

"Mine," I growled, my control slipping.

They snapped around her thighs, leaving light-red marks. She stared at me with wide eyes, then hurried toward my office door.

"I'm sorry," she said breathlessly. "I shouldn't have come. This was wrong."

I wanted to tell her that none of this was wrong, that I was just about to lose control, but I couldn't speak again without knowing that my wolf wouldn't say anything to her or transform. So, I let her slip out and shut the door behind her.

As soon as she disappeared, I growled and grabbed my desk, drawing my claws across the top of it to please my wolf a bit. Something to distract him, something to keep him here so he wouldn't run after Bria.

Though ... I could still smell her. Everything was so much more intensified.

"Find mate now."

Growling again, I flipped the desk, pulled books off shelves, stuffed my nose in *The Red Hammer* that she returned earlier. I needed to make sure that I gave Bria enough time to get back home safe before I ran out of here.

Run.

I needed to run. I needed to get off this campus. I needed to get away.

If I stayed here a moment longer, I'd follow her scent back to her dorm room and do more than rip off another pair of panties to stuff into my office desk. But the way she looked without them, the way her cunt smelled, the way her silkiness felt in my hand ...

Fuck.

After checking down the halls for any human students and not sensing any, I hurried out through the halls with my canines extended far past my lips and my claws lengthened all the way. When I opened one of the many back doors, I collapsed onto all fours and transformed into my wolf, forcing myself to ignore Bria's lingering scent and run back to my pack house.

And that was what I did. I ran fucking fast through the wet forest, ignoring the foul scents around me. All I could focus on was getting home ... until I came face-to-face with Alpha Adan of the Goldtooth Pack, a vicious man who had done far worse than kill innocent humans to get what he wanted. And now, he was on my land, wanting something from me.

Chapter Ten

BRIA

The library housed thousands of books, and none of them were helpful in the slightest.

I shoved another book back onto the shelf, hoping that I put it back in the right spot so that others could find it, and pulled out the next mythology book, quickly scanning the blurb for any helpful information.

When this book didn't work either, I placed it back on the bookshelf and yawned.

I hadn't slept.

Since nine p.m. last night, I had paced my small dorm room and wondered what I had done wrong. What happened within those few moments? At first, Professor Lee had been so freaking adamant about pleasing me, and then, right when I was about to come, he demanded that I leave and not turn back.

Maybe he really understood what he was doing.

Maybe he realized that he screwed up by touching a student.

Maybe he—gah, I didn't know. I didn't understand it one freaking bit. He had been so possessive, so needy, and so dominant last night when he tossed me up onto his desk, ripped off my panties, and called my pussy his.

What changed?

Deciding that I would never know, I stepped back to scan the next higher shelf. I jumped up onto my toes to check for the book I had been searching for since six a.m. this morning because last night, while I lay on Professor Lee's desk in a complete mess, I swore I saw something I had only read about in mythology books.

After three more books, I finally pulled down a book that fit my search almost perfectly. I sighed in relief, checking the time and realizing that I would be late to mythology. I didn't really want to go back to Lee's class after what had happened last night, but I didn't want to miss a class.

It really wasn't like me, and I needed not to fail this semester.

I couldn't go back home to Mom and Dad.

At the checkout, the overworked, under-caffeinated college kid with unkempt black hair grabbed the book from me. "Greek mythology, huh?" he asked, scanning the barcode and punching in a couple buttons on the computer. "I don't remember Professor Lee assigning this when I was in his class."

My heart raced a bit faster at the sound of his name. "How'd you know I take mythology with Lee?"

He cracked the brightest smile he could for it being a couple minutes before eight a.m.. "He's the only professor to teach mythology at the university. Plus, no other classics teacher would even think about having their students read *The Legend of Lycaon*. They're all too old and love Homer too much."

"True," I said, keeping up some small talk.

Once I grabbed the book from him, I held it to my chest and walked out of the library doors, heading straight for Classics with Professor Lee. While this book might've been related to mythology, I didn't get it for his class. I got it because last night, I swore I saw something in Profesor Lee's eyes that was unexplainable.

Every few moments, his eyes would flicker to a yellow-gold.

And every article, every social media post, every WebMD diagnosis told me that wasn't possible for a human. And ... I mean, I was probably overthinking this and making things up ... but I felt like I had read something about eyes shifting colors in mythology before.

Opening the book, I swept through the first few pages and walked toward the classics building, a cold wind chilling my skin. I pulled my light fall jacket closer around my body and looked up briefly to see Levi walking out from the forest, his hair a disheveled mess and his eyes glowing gold.

I sucked in a sharp breath, snapped my book closed, and stepped behind a building, staring at him with wide eyes as he slung a backpack over his shoulder and walked toward the classics building, biceps swelling through his T-shirt under the early morning sunlight.

How wasn't he freezing cold?

I stared like a creep for a few more moments as Levi disappeared into the classics building. I stepped back onto the walkway, blew out a deep breath—telling myself that I was sleep-deprived—and walked toward the classics building.

The closer I came to the entrance doors, the heavier my feet became. I didn't want to come here today. I wanted to slip back into my dorm room and sleep for the rest of the day, skipping all my damn classes.

My stomach was in tight knots, the thought of confronting Professor Lee making me uneasy. What would I even say to him? Would he even want to talk to me? Would he acknowledge it? What if he didn't?

Gosh, this was going to be even more awkward than I imagined all night.

About twenty feet ahead, Jasmine walked up the steps and through the classics building door. I stopped dead in my tracks and sucked in another sharp breath, nerves running up and down my spine and my breath catching.

What was she doing here?

She didn't even take any mythology or classics courses. Hell, the closest building she had a class in was the science building, which was about a quarter mile west of here. She wouldn't step in this building if she didn't ...

Fuck.

I balled my hands into tight fists and gritted my teeth together.

If she switched into Lee's class ...

Unable to stop myself, I pushed my nerves to the side and hurried up the steps behind her, rushing toward the mythology classroom and stopping before the double doors. Even from here, I could smell the vanilla perfume that she doused herself in every morning.

"No," I whispered to myself. "No. She can't."

After blowing out a deep breath, I looked around the doorframe and into the class.

Jasmine stood at the front of the class with a skimpy, cropped tank top that showed off her toned, tanned abs and a grin that stretched from ear to ear. After tucking some hair behind her ear, she said something that I couldn't quite hear to Professor Lee, which granted her a smile from him. A fucking smile.

Those lips that had told me to leave his office last night were smiling at Jasmine.

I balled my hands into fists, tears welling up in my eyes, and walked back to my dorm room to read. All this time, I thought that ... that I meant something to him. But that was my fault to believe something that could never be true.

Professor Lee had made a mistake last night. And there was only one way to make sure that I was never his mistake again—I was going to switch out of his class.

Chapter Eleven

CALLUM

Where the fuck was Bria?

I paced around the front of my classroom to lecture about Ovid, but I couldn't get my mind off of Bria or what happened last night. Every time the door opened or a pen fell or a paper flipped on someone's desk, I looked up at the exit doors to see if it was Bria Benton.

She didn't seem like the type of girl to skip class.

From the moment I met her, she seemed very particular and anxious about missing any sort of event, had stumbled into the classics building in a rush and a complete mess of nerves, hair crazy from the wind and eyes wide in fear that she'd be late.

"Professor Lee?" Jasmine said, sitting in Bria's seat in the front row.

After cursing to myself, I stood behind the podium and rubbed my sweaty palms together, giving her a nod to ask whatever kind of question she had for me now. She had been the only person asking questions all class. And while I would find it refreshing on any other day, I couldn't think straight now.

Between Bria and Alpha Adan showing up on my property, I hadn't shut my eyes to sleep once last night. He had threatened me with war if I didn't find him information on a new student at the university, and normally, I would gladly accept war with someone like him.

But I had Bria to worry about now.

And she still hadn't shown up.

"Can you give us your opinion on mythology in pop culture?" Jasmine asked.

I blew a steady breath through my nose so as to not come off as pissed off to my other students and gave her a tense smile. "Maybe some other time. We have an exam in a couple weeks and need to get through this material."

"An exam already?" she asked, the rest of the class starting to groan about it.

"Yes, Jasmine," I said, wanting nothing more than to scold her through our mind link.

Once I guided the class back into the material, I finished my lecture early, placed my hands on either side of the podium, and tightened my grip until the students started to pile out of the classroom. My mind reeled with thoughts, worries, scenarios about what could've happened to Bria.

What if someone tipped Alpha Adan off that I had been paying special attention to Bria? What if he took her as collateral until I found him that fucking information? Which I wouldn't, but I needed to at least make it seem like I was until I could come up with a plan. He had our pack and this school surrounded.

After class, Jasmine walked up to me with a grin on her face. "Professor Lee, I—"

"Where's Bria?" I asked bluntly, unable to hold myself back any longer.

Jasmine might've been part of my pack, but my mate was somewhere on campus, thinking that I pushed her away last night because I was a shitty person. I needed to talk to her, and I needed to talk to her now. I didn't care where she was. I would hunt her down.

"I don't know," Jasmine said. "I, um, matter of fact, I haven't seen her since yesterday."

"You haven't seen her since yesterday?" I growled. "Why didn't you tell me?"

She widened her eyes even more and shook her head. "I didn't know that you wanted to know about her. She's just a human. There are tons of girls like her in this school. I ... I ..." She furrowed her brows and glanced back up at me. "Oh my Goddess, she's your mate, isn't she?"

Pressing my lips together, I closed my eyes and blew out a breath. I didn't want anyone to find out yet. I had Adan and the council to worry about, and I needed to keep Bria safe. But ... it was difficult to keep something like this a secret to everyone around, especially when Bria was my mate.

"Yes, she's my mate," I said, lowering my voice so nobody else would hear.

Jasmine straightened out her shoulders, pulled up her shirt to cover her breasts, and looked down at her feet. "Sorry, I didn't know. If I had, I wouldn't have ... um, switched into your class or, um ..."

"It's fine, Jasmine. I ..." I rubbed a hand across my face. "I need you to watch and protect her for me. If you find her today, please tell me. I haven't seen her since last night, and we have a pack on our borders, ready to attack."

Jasmine nodded. "I'll let you know, Alpha."

And with that, she turned on her heel and hurried up the auditorium steps. Beta Milo cleared his throat and waited by the door. Jasmine passed him and bowed her head, scurrying down the hallway.

I snapped my textbook shut, on edge and needing to find Bria to make sure that she was safe. I didn't want to deal with pack drama right now or Alpha Adan; I needed to be with her. She drove me fucking crazy without even trying.

"What's wrong?" I asked, running a hand through my hair.

"Alpha Adan is looking for one of your students."

My stomach tightened in knots. "Who?"

"Bria Benton."

Chapter Twelve

BRIA

Professor Lee.

I read his name on his office door over and over again, my palms becoming sweatier by the second. I shouldn't have come here, but I couldn't stop myself. I wanted to prove to myself that Callum Lee, my professor, didn't really like me. What happened between us was nothing more than a measly hookup. If I told him I was transferring out of his class, then he would shrug his shoulders and say that he didn't care.

Though … I should've come during his office hours while there were other students around. Not now, when the halls were emptying out and Professor Lee was probably alone behind this door.

When I went to knock, I stopped myself. What if he wasn't alone and was with another student, like Jasmine, doing to her what he had done to me yesterday? If I walked in on that or interrupted him and saw someone else, I would—

"Thank fuck," Professor Lee said from behind me.

My eyes widened, and I twirled around. Lee stood at the end of the hallway, releasing a heavy breath, with his large shoulders slumped forward and creases in his forehead. At the sight of him, I swallowed hard and stepped out of the way of his office.

I didn't know what to say, or how to say it, or if I should say anything.

So, I stood there with my book held to my chest and my heart thumping against my rib cage. He stalked closer to me, his hazel eyes intensifying by the moment. When he reached me, he unlocked his office door and nodded for me to walk into the room.

"We need to talk."

After scurrying into the room like some sort of prey, I stood by his door awkwardly. He walked around his desk and sat down, his jaw clenched but his stare never leaving mine. "Where were you during class, Miss Benton?"

"Ms. Benton?" I asked, suddenly taken aback.

He tightened his fists on the table. "Answer my question."

"No. I don't have to tell you where I was. It's not like you'd care anyway," I said, anger and jealousy rushing through me. "Not when you have Jasmine in your class now. I'm surprised that you even noticed I was gone."

When his fists came down hard on the desk, I jumped.

He stood, looming over the place where he had knelt between my legs last night and tasted me. "Of course I noticed that you were gone, Bria. Where were you? Why didn't you tell me that you weren't coming to class?"

Reeling and hurt, I stared at Professor Lee. "Why did you tell me to leave last night?"

Professor Lee tensed, the anger slowly fading from his face. After unclenching his fists, he set them by his sides and sat back down, sighing through his nose. "Bria, it's not that simple. I ..."

"It's okay," I said. "That's not what I came here to talk about anyway. I wanted to tell you that I'm ..." I sucked in a deep breath and parted my lips. The first few times, no words came out, but then I finally forced myself to say it. "I'm switching out of your class."

All softness in his expression fell, dark brows furrowing together angrily. "No."

"I've already emailed my advisor and told her that I'm switching into Wallace's class."

Lie.

I hadn't emailed my advisor yet. I had the email open on my laptop but hadn't been able to actually click the Send button. Truth was, I didn't want to leave Lee's class. I'd do anything to stay, but—this was so stupid because Professor Lee didn't even like me like that—seeing him with Jasmine made me so angry. I couldn't do that every day.

Hell, I was a freshman in college. I should be enjoying my life, not getting anxiety over a crush that would go absolutely nowhere. It was forbidden for me and him to even do what we did.

So, I turned on my heel, away from an angry Professor Lee, and walked toward the door. Every step was harder than the last, my legs physically becoming heavier by the moment. I couldn't understand it for the life of me—why I was so drawn to him—but I didn't stop walking. I made it all the way to the door, turned the handle, and opened it only a few inches.

Professor Lee smacked his large, callous hand across the door, snapping it shut, and shoved me against it, his nose trailing up the side of my neck and his warm breath sending chills down my spine.

"You're not leaving me," Lee growled into my ear. "You're mine."

My breath hitched, pussy clenching at his words.

You're mine.

Two little words that made me feel all sorts of things that I really shouldn't.

"You're not walking out of here without me making your pussy fucking cry all over my fingers," he said, teeth grazing against my neck.

Before I could react, Callum shoved two fingers into my pants and between my pussy lips, rubbing my wet, aching, and needy cunt.

I dug my fingers into the door until they turned white and bit my lip to hold back my whimpers. It was all so sudden and so quickly that the book, *The Legend of Lycaon*, slipped from my hands and onto the ground.

Professor Lee tensed, then kicked it under his bookcase, fingers slipping inside of me so quickly that it was almost inhuman. Every time his fingers entered me, my pussy made sloppy, wet sounds for him and tightened even more.

"I want to be inside of you so bad," he growled against me, his teeth gliding against my neck.

I clenched and spread my legs even wider, arching my back. "Please, Professor, please, fuck me. It's all I have been able to think about these past few days. I ... I've touched myself one too many times, thinking about you inside of me."

A monstrous sound exited his throat, his hands becoming rougher by the moment. I went to turn around, but he held me in place, rubbing and fucking my pussy raw with his fingers until my juices actually started running down my thighs.

Wanting to touch him, I reached behind me to place my fingers on his cheek, dragging them through his thick facial hair and down his lips. He growled, ground his cock against me from behind, and rubbed my clit. I drew my fingers against his bottom lip, the side of my pointer finger gliding against his teeth, which were elongated, so large and thick and came to a point sharp enough to break skin.

My breath hitched again, and I went to turn around to see what it was, but Callum held me in place.

"Don't move," he said, breathing heavily against me and slipping his fingers into my pussy, bicep flexing against my side.

The pressure rose in my core; I was so close to orgasming by him. This wasn't as good as last night—when he had his mouth on my cunt and his beard decorated with my juices—but, gosh, it was fucking amazing.

"Kiss me," I breathed, wanting to feel more of him all over me.

"I can't," he said tensely.

"Please."

"No," he growled.

Though I was so close and I wanted it so bad, I … I didn't understand this. I didn't know what he wanted from me. He said that he wanted to fuck me, but he didn't want to kiss me. He said that he didn't regret last night, but now, he didn't even want to look me in the eye.

Anger rushing through me, I shoved myself off the door and twirled around. Professor Lee growled louder this time, the sound so inhuman that it both scared me and made me clench, and turned around to face his desk.

"What is wrong with you?" I asked, brows furrowed together. "Why don't you want to see me?"

Professor Lee placed his hands on his desk, every muscle flexing through the back of his shirt. "Bria, it's not that I don't want to see you."

"Then, why can't you turn around and face me?" I asked, brows furrowed together and heart pounding inside my chest. "Why can't you look me in the eye after what happened between us last night? If you didn't regret it—"

"I don't regret it," Lee said harshly, the wooden desk snapping under his fingers. "Stop saying that."

"No!" I crossed my arms over my chest, on the verge of tears because I was tired and upset.

I shouldn't have flirted with him. I shouldn't have visited him during office hours. I shouldn't have let him eat me out last night. I was less than a week into college, and I was fucked up over this man —over my damn professor!—for no reason at all already.

Turning around, I faced the door and grabbed the handle. What was wrong with me? I wanted him so badly that it hurt me to leave; I didn't even have the damn strength to turn the knob and walk right out on him. I fucking wanted him, and it messed me up more than I thought it would.

Another moment passed.

Lee shuffled behind me, placed his hand on my waist, and ... pulled me closer to him, pressing his nose to my neck and inhaling sharply. "I don't regret it, Bria," he whispered into my ear. "I would never regret you."

I stared at the door, hand tightening around the knob. "Then, why?"

"I'm trying to protect you."

"Are you trying to protect me or protect yourself?" I asked, pressing my lips together.

If someone found out about us, he'd get in trouble too. He'd be kicked out of the school and wouldn't be able to teach anymore. He made it seem like this was all for me, but ... it was to protect his ass.

Before I could react, Callum turned me around, took my face into his hands, and kissed me hard, really kissed me. I sucked in a breath, in shock, and found myself relaxing under his touch. When he pulled away from me, he rested his forehead against mine.

"I'd rather have you than keep my job, Bria." He pushed some hair behind my ear. "You're not leaving my class. You're going to show up every morning bright and early, so I can see this beautiful face of yours sitting in my front row. And you don't have a choice in that, honey. You're mine."

Chapter Thirteen

CALLUM

"Yours," Bria whispered, fiddling with the buttons on my shirt. "I'm ... yours."

Listening to the words come out of her mouth made me feel so good. I had waited forty-three years to find my mate, forty-three long, lonely years. And I so desperately wanted to really have her, wanted to sink my teeth into her pretty neck and claim her as my own.

But she was a human.

She'd need time to adjust to the reality of me being a man who could transform into a feral, savage, violent wolf. She'd need even more time to make that shift herself. Plenty of humans didn't survive their first transformation, and I wanted to make my Bria strong enough. I couldn't lose her.

"You're mine," I repeated.

"Only yours?" she asked again, her breath hitching.

"Only mine."

"But I'm your student."

And she was my mate too, but I couldn't tell her that. She wouldn't understand. Not yet.

"That doesn't make a difference to me," I said, taking her chin in my hand and forcing her to look up at me with those big, beautiful eyes. "I will have you, no matter who you are to me, no matter who tries to take you away from me, no matter what." I moved closer to her to whisper in her ear, "You will forever be mine."

After inhaling sharply, Bria shuffled awkwardly between me and the door and tried to hide a grin. I could smell her cunt again. She loved this. She loved the mere thought of her being mine forever and always.

I'd be lying if I said I didn't love it too.

Her phone buzzed, and she jumped up in surprise. "I have to get to my next class."

Reluctantly, I stepped away from her, leaned against my desk, and crossed my arms over my chest. "We have a quiz tomorrow. You'd better be in class bright and early, Bria, or else I'll come and find you."

Bria pressed her lips together to suppress a smile. "And do what?"

A growl escaped my lips, which made Bria widen her eyes in excitement. "Or I'll drag you back here from your dorm room and lay you over my knee."

Cheeks flushing red, she grasped the door handle. "I guess I'll sleep in tomorrow."

My lips curled into a smirk. The thought of Bria lying across my lap with my hand smacking her ass until it was red made me hard. She would be in class tomorrow, but one day, I was sure that I'd get to spank her until her pussy was sopping fucking wet for me.

Just as she was about to exit the room, she paused and glanced under my shelf. "Can I have my library book back?"

After glancing under the shelf, I tensed when I saw *The Legend of Lycaon* glimmering under the dark shelf like an ancient artifact aching to be found. Picking it up, I held it in my hands and gestured toward it. "Why do you want this?"

This wasn't just any book.

This was a Greek mythology book about the first lycan.

Bria inhaled sharply and chewed on the inside of her lip, making eye contact with me for the briefest moment but then looking away as if she was afraid of what I'd say or what I'd do. "Because I do ..."

"For a class?"

"No."

"For pleasure?"

"Kinda ..."

I handed the book back to her after a couple moments. She took it from me and held it to her chest, swallowing hard and glancing back up at me. With that, she opened the door and walked out.

At the very last moment, she turned around and threw me a smile over her shoulder. "And, Professor Lee, I never switched out of your class."

She disappeared down the hall and around the corner. I stood in my office with my lips pulled into a smile. Bria knew exactly what she was doing when she showed up at my office with that book in her hands. She wanted me to get angry, to get possessive and jealous. She got what she wanted.

When I heard the classics building door close, I locked my office door and followed Bria's scent. Danger still lingered on this campus, and I wouldn't let Alpha Adan take my mate, especially now that I was so fucking close to having her.

Bria walked through the quad, waving to a couple people, including Levi, then walked through the English building doors. I watched her disappear into the building and marched up to Levi, who lay on the grass with his shirt off and a pair of sunglasses on his face.

"What's up?" he asked me, leaning back on his elbows and crossing his ankles.

"I need you to keep an eye on Bria," I said through clenched teeth even though I absolutely hated the thought of it. It was less suspicious if Levi and Jasmine were watching her too, especially when I needed to teach class or had pack business to take care of.

Levi lifted his sunglasses to his forehead. "You're serious?"

"Yes."

"I thought you wanted me to stay away from her."

"I don't want you touching her or flirting with her," I snapped. "But I need you to protect her. Alpha Adan is getting closer to the university, and he's looking for her. You and Jasmine are the only people who know Bria and who I trust to keep her safe."

Brows drawn together, Levi paused for a couple moments, then tensed. "Goddess, she's our lu—"

I growled to shut him up really quick. "Don't fucking say it out loud," I scolded. "I don't know who is listening and working for Adan. All I need you and Jasmine to do is protect her while I'm not around."

Levi stood and nodded. "You can count on me."

Narrowing my eyes, I arched a brow at him. "No flirting."

"No flirting."

"No touching."

"No touching," Levi repeated.

The thought of anyone touching my mate made me more than rageful.

Unable to stop myself, I wrapped my hand around his neck and let my canines lengthen enough for him to see them. "If I find out that you have done either or let *anyone* do either to her, I will personally rip your throat out and feed it to you."

My words came out harsh, but I couldn't help them. Bria was my mate, who would only ever be with me. She wouldn't be touched by another man.

"Bria's mine."

Chapter Fourteen

BRIA

For dinner, Jasmine and I sat at a high-top table at Lunar Chamber, a college restaurant about a block from campus. Jasmine sipped on a lemonade, eyeing a couple of alcoholic drinks our waiter brought another group of students.

She nudged me. "You think if I flirt with him, he'd bring us some?"

I arched a brow, annoyance bubbling inside me. "I thought you were set on flirting with Professor Lee?"

Don't get me wrong; I was all for her flirting with whoever she wanted, but I was still pissed off at her that she switched into Lee's class to flirt with him. He had told me that I was his and would forever be his, but ... sometimes, people lied to get what they wanted. My parents had made sure I knew that.

Though I didn't think he would lie to me too—he seemed genuine—I didn't like the thought of my roommate being all over him. If I was his, that meant that he was mine, and I wouldn't let anyone else touch him. I hadn't ever been in a relationship like this before, had never had someone pay this much attention to me; I wasn't going to give that up.

Jasmine snorted. "Not anymore."

Sitting up taller, I glanced at her. "What do you mean?"

"Ugh." Jasmine wrinkled her nose. "I'm not interested in him. I realized that he's too old for me. Next year, he'll be wobbling around with a cane."

My lips curled into a smile, and I couldn't help but giggle at the thought of Callum Lee with a cane. He was way too ripped, walked around with way too much confidence, and looked way too sexy for that to be him next year.

Jasmine took a sip of her lemonade. "Professor Lee is all yours, Bria."

"Um, what about me?" Levi said, scooting onto the third stool. "Who gets me?"

Jasmine choked on her drink and held a hand to her chest. "I know you did not just say that."

Levi wiggled his eyebrows at her. "You know I did, babe."

Jasmine kicked him in the shin underneath the table with the tip of her high heel.

He grunted and tensed, raising his brows and looking down at the table. "Damn, I deserved that." After a moment of recovery, Levi looked over at me. "What are you ladies up to?"

"Jasmine wanted to—"

Curling her arm around my shoulders, Jasmine pulled me closer. "Talking about how Bria wants to ride Professor Lee."

My eyes widened, cheeks flushing. I smacked Jasmine in the shoulder and glared at her, not wanting the entire world to find out that I liked him, especially like that. I hadn't told Jasmine what happened between us, but I didn't want any rumors flying around campus.

"Same though," Levi said, sitting back and grabbing a beer from the waiter.

Lips curling into a wider smile, I laughed and grabbed a fry from my plate. "I don't know if Professor Lee likes you back, Levi," I teased. "He kept glaring at you all class yesterday. I was scared that he'd rip your throat out."

Levi chuckled tensely and scratched the back of his head. "Yeah, rip out my throat ..."

Jasmine bumped her shoulder into mine. "Maybe you can make your move on him during the Full Moon party next Friday."

"The Full Moon party will be the perfect time," Levi said, stealing a fry from my plate and nodding to Jasmine with a sly smirk on his face. "He won't be able to resist her then; he'll turn into a wild animal."

Again, Jasmine kicked Levi in the shin. I furrowed my brows at the intense and silent exchange between the two. Levi seemed like the type of guy to spill a bit too much information, which could definitely be useful at some point ... maybe.

"What's a Full Moon party?"

"During the first full moon of the school year, the university throws a party for new freshmen to celebrate." Levi leaned back and glanced around the room. "Last year, the party was a rager."

The waiter came over with the checks, and I handed him a few dollars, then I slid off the chair and walked with Jasmine and Levi toward the exit. People waved to Jasmine and Levi as we walked by, slapping them on their backs like they had known them for years.

Jasmine looped her arm around mine and pushed through the doors, stepping into the crisp fall night. I inched closer to her, freezing at the wind, which she seemed to be fine with, even in a tank top and some shorts.

"You have to go," Jasmine said. "It's so fun."

"You've been before?" I asked.

"My friends and I used to sneak into the party while we were still in high school."

"You live around here?"

"We both do," Levi said, shoving his hands into his jeans pockets. "Many of the students that go here come from around the forest that surrounds the university. That's why we know the majority of them."

"Oh," I said, brows furrowed. "I didn't think that there were that many communities around here. The school seems pretty secluded."

Levi and Jasmine shared another tense glance, then Jasmine cleared her throat.

"It is," she said. "We live a bit south, about forty-five minutes from here."

Suddenly, howls erupted through the forest. I tensed and found myself stopping and gazing into the dark woods, my heart pounding in my chest. Another howl sounded, then another. It sounded like ... a pack of wolves.

Jasmine tugged on my wrist a bit harder and dragged me toward our dorm with Levi in tow. "Let's get back inside. It's getting late, and don't you have to be up early for Professor Lee's class? You don't want to miss too many classes or else he'll deduct some points."

I chewed on the inside of my lip. "Are there wolves around here?"

Both Levi and Jasmine stayed quiet.

Levi finally nodded and opened the front dorm door for me. "Yeah, some. I've seen them around here for a few years now, but usually, they're not dangerous."

A loud yowl sounded through the dark forest.

"Not dangerous?" I whispered.

That sounded like one of them was in pain and lots of it, like one attacked the other—or worse ... one attacked a student.

Jasmine pulled me into the stuffy building and waved Levi off. "See you tomorrow."

After a couple moments, Levi rounded the building's corner and disappeared into the night, heading right for the noise. I swallowed hard and watched him run off. Something wasn't right, and I wanted to find out what it was.

Chapter Fifteen

CALLUM

"*Alpha Lee,"* Milo said through the mind link. *"We're tracking Alpha Adan. He's approaching university grounds. We need you to meet us at the northeastern borders, so he doesn't harm any students."*

I tensed and stood from my desk, gazing out into the hallway to make sure nobody else was around. Just as I was about to end the fucking day, this asshole had to show up. And I hoped to the Goddess that Bria was still with Jasmine, like Jasmine had told me she was earlier.

Running out into the darkness, I surveyed the woods once more and shifted into my wolf, sprinting toward the northeastern borders to meet my pack and to stop Adan from advancing farther onto university lands.

When I saw him standing among his warriors, I growled harshly and shifted into my human again, smelling my pack close behind. "You're not moving any farther onto the university."

Adan turned around, eyes a blazing gold.

"Bria Benton," Alpha Adan growled. "I need to find her."

"Why do you want Benton?"

I asked the question like her name didn't affect me, like I didn't know who she was.

But, Goddess, I did.

If Adan found out that Bria was my mate, then things would get a whole lot worse for us very quickly. I needed to keep Bria safe from everything that she didn't even know about yet.

"That's none of your fucking business." He moved closer to me with his claws drawn. "Where is she?"

Hands balled into fists, I stepped closer to him to show him and his pack that I wasn't afraid of him because I wasn't. My pack could defeat him easily. But we were on school grounds with humans less than half a mile from us, and Bria's dorm was close. Too close.

"I already fucking told you that I don't know who she is."

"And I thought I made it clear that you needed to find her."

"I don't take orders from anyone, Adan."

Growling, Adan leaped into the air and shifted into his wolf, rushing at me. I shifted into mine, spotting my warriors approaching their pack from behind. And before I knew it, the forest turned into a bloodbath with fur flying everywhere, the needle-covered path becoming a river of thick wolf blood and howls drifting through the air.

We fought for what must've been almost an hour until Adan lifted his nose in the air and howled. His wolves retreated through the woods, and I almost wanted to follow after him to end this all right here and right now, but I ...

I smelled Bria's scent drifting through the woods.

She was close.

If Adan found her ...

After ordering my wolves to get home safely so we could come up with a plan, I ran toward her scent. From a distance, I spotted Bria standing out on the quad all by her-fucking-self. It must've been one in the morning already, and Alpha Adan was searching for her. I didn't know if he knew what she looked like or smelled like, but I wasn't taking any chances, so I shifted behind a tree.

"What are you doing out here, Bria?" I scolded, rushing toward her, completely naked because my clothes were stuffed in the bush behind her.

She must've thought I was fucking insane, stalking at her bare and covered in blood, but it didn't matter. I needed her out of here fast. Alpha Adan was on my ass about finding her as quickly as supernaturally possible.

"Professor Lee," Bria said in a breathy whisper. With wide eyes, she took her time, glancing down my naked body, her mouth forming a small O. "Wh-what are you ..." When her gaze reached my cock hanging between my thighs, her cheeks turned bright red. "Oh my ..."

I snatched her upper arm and dragged her into the classics building, slamming and locking the door behind me. After bringing her to my office and locking the door, in case that asshole smelled us, I finally released her.

Rubbing her arm, she looked everywhere, except at me. "I just needed some fresh air."

"You could've gotten fresh air outside of your dorm. Why'd you come all the way here?"

She gnawed on the inside of her cheek and glanced down at my junk again. "Because ..." After crossing her legs and rubbing them together, the scent of her cunt coming off her in waves, she turned away and shuffled toward the window. "I ... smelled something good ... um, you. Is that weird?" She groaned and rubbed a hand over her face. "Gosh, it's even weirder to say out loud."

Rummaging through my closet, I pulled out some spare clothes and tugged them on. Then, stepping closer to her, I gripped her waist from behind. "It's not weird," I murmured into her ear.

To a human, it might've been.

But this was the mate bond taking full effect. It was so strong that it even affected humans.

She stayed quiet for a long time, then cleared her throat. "Why're you covered in blood?" she asked me, voice tense and awaiting an answer. Yet she didn't turn around to face me again. It was almost as if she was scared.

I swallowed hard, wanting to desperately tell her what I was and what she meant to me. It had barely been a fucking week, and my mate was driving me so fucking crazy. I wanted to keep her safe any way possible, and keeping this quiet until Alpha Adan went away was best.

The more she knew, the less safe she was.

"That's a story for another day."

"Are you okay?"

"Yes, Bria," I said, dragging my nose up the side of her neck and inhaling her sweet scent. My shoulders slumped forward at the smell, relaxing me down to my very core. I had never experienced so many emotions from a single scent before.

Bria remained quiet for a couple more moments, her body tense in front of me.

"What's wrong?" I murmured into her ear.

"I ..." She paused and curled her fingers against the windowsill. "I have another question."

"About what?"

"Mythology."

"What is it, Bria? You can ask me anything."

She turned around and stared deeply into my eyes with her intense ones. Nervously, she gulped and chewed on her lip. "Do you believe in supernatural creatures, like ... lycans and werewolves?"

Chapter Sixteen

BRIA

I didn't even mean to ask Callum about lycans and werewolves. The words seemed to tumble out of my mouth. But now that I had said them out loud, I so desperately wanted his answer because some things weren't adding up.

Professor Lee stared down at me with wide hazel eyes. Instead of telling me that all the fantasies in my head were true, he let out a small chuckle, the deep sound making me warm in all the right places. "Where did you hear that?"

"I ... I've just been reading," I whispered.

"Did you finish *The Legend of Lycaon*?"

"Yes."

"Did you like it?"

"Yes."

"Did you—"

"Why aren't you answering my question?" I asked.

Again, Professor Lee widened his eyes and ran a hand through his scruff. If there was anything I learned in that book, it was that some wolves—especially male wolves, the alpha type—didn't like to be confronted and didn't like disobedience.

Lee liked neither.

Still, I could barely believe werewolves existed myself. The thought was so outlandish that it was laughable. If werewolves existed, surely, the government would've discovered them by now. I didn't think *any* government would be okay with having supernatural creatures roaming around.

"In Greek mythology, I think people believed in—"

"No," I said, somehow and somewhere finding the courage to talk back to him. "I want to know what you think about them here and now. Not in Greek mythology. In today's time period and in today's world. Do you think they exist?"

Callum stared at me for a few moments, jaw twitching and a sudden flash of gold in his eyes. After stepping away from me, he glanced at his desk. "Why would I believe in something like that, Bria?"

"So, you don't think they're real?" I asked, moving closer.

Part of me wanted him to break. After finishing that mythology book about wolves, I researched online and found a whole slew of dirty, smutty romance books about werewolves, especially alpha wolves, and I might've ... touched myself while reading a couple.

A couple of silently tense moments passed between us. The heat grew between my legs as I thought back to those books—the violent and vicious nature of a man who grew claws and canines during a full moon, the possessive claiming and marking on another, the pure aggression that every wolf had.

Fuck.

They were all made-up stories, but I couldn't stop thinking about them. Truth was that I kinda wished that Professor Lee would snap and show me his canines, sink them into my neck, and take me. That'd be the damn highlight of my entire life.

"No," Professor Lee finally said, but he was lying.

He couldn't look me in the eye anymore.

"So, you don't believe in people who can lengthen their stubby nails into sharp claws?"

"No."

"What about people who can extend their teeth into viciously long canines?"

"No."

"And their eyes?" I said, my voice lower. "It might be easy for someone to hide claws in balled fists or canines behind their lips, but eyes that change to gold ..." The more I said, the harder my heart pounded. "Nobody can hide their eyes changing colors."

"Eyes don't change colors, Miss Benton." Callum placed his hands on the desk, every muscle in his back flexing so hard that I wanted to run my hands all over his taut body. "It's impossible."

But it wasn't.

Professor Lee wasn't the only man whose eyes flashed gold that I'd seen.

Adan had eyes like that too.

"You should get back to your dorm, Bria," Professor Lee said, grabbing a shirt from his closet and holding open the door for me. After he tugged the shirt over his head, he followed me out of the room and down the hallway. "We have a quiz tomorrow morning. I hope that you studied."

He thought he was good at changing the conversation.

"Yeah," I said, playing along with him. "I did."

"You have to make up your quiz from today too."

"Can I do that in office hours?" I asked, moving closer to him when we stepped out into the chilly fall night. Goose bumps rose on my skin, and I wrapped my arms around myself to keep warm.

Professor Lee chuckled lowly. "I don't have office hours tomorrow."

"You wouldn't open them up for me?"

Hell, I didn't know where all this confidence was coming from, but I liked it. And I couldn't stop flirting with him. Every day that passed, I felt the need to be closer to him, for him to take me, for him to crave me.

Maybe I was ... lonely from all the years I spent by myself back at home.

This was the first real thing I had.

When we approached my dorm building, Professor Lee stared at me with those beautiful hazel eyes that seemed to twinkle under the moonlight. "I don't make special requests, Miss Benton. Not usually."

"But for me?"

He smiled and turned away. "I'll set aside an evening for you, Bria. Anytime."

* * *

When I made it up to the dorm room, I heard two voices inside, so I stopped and pressed my ear to the door.

"Lee is going to kill us," Jasmine whisper-yelled behind our door. "What are we going to do? Where could she have gone off to? She barely leaves the dorm room to go anywhere! Why would she just—"

Suddenly, Jasmine stopped, and I backed away from the door.

Fuck.

Had she caught me?

A moment later, the door swung open.

"Bria!" Jasmine scolded when I walked back into my dorm room. When I left, she had been sleeping soundly, but now, Levi sat on her bed as she ran over to me, worried. "Where the hell have you been?"

"I was"—I shifted from foot to foot—"out."

"You can't go out at two in the morning!" Jasmine said, teeth grinding together. "Something could've happened to you. If you're going to go out, tell me before you leave. I'll come with you."

"I didn't want to wake you."

"Well, don't do that again, please."

Levi hopped off Jasmine's bed and walked over to me, brows

drawn together. He took a couple strands of my hair in his hand and sniffed me—freaking sniffed me like a dog would. "You've been out with Professor Lee."

It wasn't a question. It was a statement.

Levi glanced over his shoulder at Jasmine, and for the second time tonight, they shared a silent look that I couldn't decipher. I pulled my hair away from him and marched over to my bed, kicked off my shoes and wiggled out of my jeans. I was too tired to get scolded by my friends.

"Whoa! Whoa! Whoa! Whoa! Whoa!" Levi covered his eyes with his hands. "You can't strip in front of me. He'll kill me if I—"

Jasmine elbowed him hard in the ribs and jumped onto her bed, looking way more relaxed than she had a couple moments ago. "Were you out with Professor Lee?" she asked, wiggling her eyebrows at me.

I pulled on some sweatpants. "Maybe."

"Girl, details! Now!" Jasmine said even though it was two in the morning and we had class bright and early tomorrow in Professor Lee's Classics class.

I both wanted to spill everything and tell her nothing.

Professor Lee was mine, and I didn't want to share any details about him with anyone else.

Once I dressed in my pajamas, Levi finally pulled his hands away from his face, said something about not wanting to lose his eyes, and jumped on Jasmine's bed with her. "You know what they were probably doing." He winked, causing Jasmine to scrunch her nose.

"Can you not?"

"What?" Levi said.

"Don't be weird."

"How am I being weird?"

"We haven't had sex," I said sharply.

But, damn, did I want to.

Levi's mouth dropped open. "You haven't?"

"No."

He threw his head back and chuckled. "Oh my Goddess. What is he waiting for? If he keeps holding back, he's going to lose control during the Full Moon party." Levi smacked his hands together, as if he was happy or excited about something.

Jasmine rolled her eyes. "Ugh, why do I keep you around?"

Levi wiggled his brows. "Because you love me, babe."

She shoved him off her bed. "Don't call me that."

"Has, um ..." I gnawed on the inside of my cheek and lay back on my bed, staring up at the ceiling. My chest tightened. "Do you think that he has lost control with other students before? I can't be the only one, right?"

Jasmine and Levi stayed quiet for a couple moments.

When I looked over at them, Levi shook his head. "I'm only a second-year student, but ... when I took his class last year, he barely spoke to anyone. Nobody really enjoys his class because it's classics. And, I mean, who likes classics?"

"I do."

"Well, of course, you do. You're his"—he paused and glanced over at an angry Jasmine—"favorite student."

Jasmine hopped off the bed, placed her hands on Levi's back, and pushed him toward the dorm room door. "Levi has to go now." She marched right out of the door with him and slammed it behind her, and they started bickering back and forth like an old couple outside.

I pulled the blankets over my head, turned onto my side, and pulled out my phone, staring down at the steamy werewolf stories that I had been reading earlier. Callum would lose control during the Full Moon party, huh?

My lips curled into a smile.

Good, because I'd do everything in my power to make that happen.

I wanted to see who the real Callum Lee was.

Chapter Seventeen

CALLUM

Throughout this past week, I had tried hard to stay away from Bria as much as I could. I didn't want any of my pack members to pick up on the fact that I paid special attention to her, as any one of them could rat me out to Alpha Adan in fear. They wouldn't, but if he threatened them with their lives, they might, and then I'd punish them.

But every fucking day that passed, it was harder to contain myself. The full moon would be here in one day—one fucking day—and I wanted so desperately to bend Bria over my desk and have my way with her. I didn't know how much longer I'd be able to last.

And, besides, Bria already knew too much.

"Remember, we have an exam on Monday on chapters five through eight in your textbook," I said, staring into the lecture hall at the hundreds of people who were way more worried about the Full Moon party on campus tomorrow night rather than a Classics exam.

I crossed my arms over my chest, eyes lingering on Bria for a moment. She gnawed on the inside of her lip and shifted in her seat, her sweet cunt almost too much to handle. Bria Benton was half my fucking age but the sexiest damn thing I had ever seen. I couldn't wait to finally have her.

My teeth ached for a moment, the way they usually did before they elongated. I had to put distance between us as soon as possible. Adan had been pushing for information all fucking week, and I ... I was fucking terrified that if I turned Bria, he'd be able to sense it.

"Class is dismissed," I said quickly. "Bria, please stay back for a moment."

Fuck. Why'd I say that?

Her eyes widened slightly as everyone started packing up their things, ready to get out of class for the weekend.

What the hell was wrong with me? As hard as I tried, as much as I needed to stay away, I couldn't. No matter what I did.

"What's he want?" Jasmine asked her, arching a brow.

She shrugged and gathered her things, pushing them into her backpack. "I'm not sure," she said, glancing over at me with those pretty eyes of hers.

I leaned against my desk, biceps flexed hard, and stared at her, feeling my eyes shift colors.

Shit.

"Well ..." Levi shoved some books in his backpack and paused as the room started to clear out. "I'll see you at the Full Moon party tomorrow."

Jasmine squealed. "I can't wait for it. It's been the talk of campus for weeks now!"

She and Levi hurried down the walkway to the doors and exited the room along with the rest of the students.

After sucking in a breath, Bria walked to the front of the room toward me. "You wanted to see me?" she asked.

And I tried so hard to keep myself calm, but her scent was drifting into my nose and making me so fucking hard.

I stared at her, the vein in my neck pulsing wildly. After a few moments, I cleared my throat and walked around the desk to gather my things, avoiding eye contact with her, but really, I just needed to hide my raging boner. "Are you prepared for the exam?"

Her brows furrowed together. "Um ... yes, I hope."

I paused and glanced up at her through the dark-framed glasses on my face. "It's going to be hard." My tongue glided against my front teeth. *Like my fucking cock when I bury it inside you.* "You should study this weekend for it. *All* weekend."

This time, she paused and nodded. "I'm planning to study all Saturday and Sunday."

I stepped closer to her and pressed my lips together. "And tomorrow night?"

"Tomorrow night, I'm going to the Full Moon party," she said.

I dug my fingers into the desk, so hard that the metal dented slightly.

"You shouldn't go," I said, needing to keep her away. "You shouldn't go to the Full Moon party."

"Why?" she asked, brows furrowed together. "It's like every other party. I'll be able to study for your class, Professor L—"

"I don't care about you studying for my class," I said, my words jarring, a warning almost.

Her eyes widened slightly at me, and I straightened myself out and cleared my throat.

"I ..." I took a deep breath. "I'm looking out for you. Those parties get wild. People don't care what they do to girls like you."

She parted her lips to say something to me, but she couldn't seem to get any words out.

"Why are you telling me this?" she finally asked, cheeks sucked in and gaze on me, looking like she would when she was sucking my—

Fuck. Fuck. Fuck. Fuck.

I tore my gaze away from her and clenched my jaw. "I'm warning you. People get ... *wild* under the full moon. It would be best if you stayed home to be safe." I paused and pulled my computer bag over my shoulder. "I will see you bright and early on Monday for our exam. Have a good weekend."

One moment passed, then two, and I wanted her to stay, but I couldn't. Instead, I gestured for her to leave the room.

She stared at me for another moment and swallowed hard, a wicked glint in her eyes. "See you on *Monday*."

* * *

On Friday night, I paced my pack house.

Bria wouldn't stay home.

She'd go to that party out of spite. She wanted me to break, and, fuck, I was going to.

But I refused to go to that party because if she wasn't out, I knew that I'd end up ripping my way into her dorm room and taking her. The moon was full, and I had no fucking control tonight. None.

Every other full moon, I could control myself. But this one was different. This one ... I had already found my mate, and I would go to great lengths to finally have her—which couldn't fucking happen with Adan lurking close by.

Milo appeared in the hallway, arms crossed over his chest. "You should rethink attending that party tonight. I know you don't want to go, but Alpha Adan has been spotted, lingering about a mile south of the universi—"

A vicious growl escaped my throat. "What?"

"Our tracker spotted him."

"No." Rage rushing through me, I balled my hands into fists and hurled one at the wall, my hand punching right through the drywall. "Fuck, no." I paced faster, my teeth elongating into canines and my claws extended. "Fuck. Bria is going to be there."

"She is there—" Milo started.

But before he could finish, I ran out the front door and shifted. The full moon took control of me and my wolf, forcing me to find Bria, ordering me to protect her, desperate for me to claim her.

And, tonight, I would.

Chapter Eighteen

BRIA

Jasmine pulled on my hand, dragging me through the crowd gathered on campus. The Full Moon party was raging with people from all classes and all years, even some graduate students. I gazed through the crowd, looking for something or maybe *someone*. Something told me to stay at home tonight, but I wanted to come out. I had been looking forward to this party since last week.

There were so many people here; it was hard to think. But Jasmine knew exactly where she was going, leading me to a group of people huddled by the woods. Though large, our campus was surrounded by acres of forest. I wouldn't be surprised if people were sneaking off into them tonight to do the same sinful things I thought about Professor Lee doing to me.

Jasmine started the night drinking a soda, and one hour later, she was dancing with the quarterback of the football team here. I stood by the edge of the forest, my arms crossed over my chest and a soda in my hand, and leaned against a tree, gnawing on the inside of my cheek. Professor Lee was right; people were going wild tonight, hormones were all over the place, people were sneaking out into the woods and were definitely *not* staying quiet.

"Babe," Levi said to my left. He pushed me against a tree, the scent of alcohol on his breath almost too much to handle, and his eyes ... they were gold. He leaned down slightly to shout in my ear because the music was way too loud. "When Professor Lee shows up, he's going to fucking destroy you."

"I don't think he's going to show," I said.

Levi brushed his nose against my ear when someone pushed into him. "Come on. You know that he will show up once you start letting loose and are having a good time." Someone bumped into him again, shoving him into me, and he snatched my hand and pulled me into the woods. "Goddess, I can't even stand out there. Come over here, where it's quieter."

I tugged back slightly. "I'm not going into the woods, where everyone bangs."

Before I could pull my hand away from him, he was torn off me —literally thrown a few meters across the woods—and landed on his back. Professor Lee stood in front of me and growled—fucking *growled.*

"She said no," he said, words so powerful.

Levi scrambled to his feet and bowed his head. "Sorry, Alpha," he said, then disappeared into the woods, clutching the back of his *bleeding* neck.

Did Lee throw him with that much force that he was bleeding?

And ... Alpha?

Professor Lee turned back to me, his eyes glowing a gold color and long teeth emerged from under his lips. He stepped closer to me, and I stepped back, hitting a tree. One hand posted above the tree, the other balled into a fist by his side, he moved closer.

"I told you to stay home."

My eyes widened, my heart pounding against my chest. His eyes should've scared me ... but I didn't feel scared at all. I fucking loved it, every single second of it. His force, aggression ... everything about it made me all hot and bothered.

All my thoughts had been true.

Werewolves were real, and one was staring back at me.

He rested his forehead against mine and let out another low growl. "Leave the party right now, Bria," he murmured against me. "You smell too fucking good. I don't know how much longer I'll be able to control myself."

Something inside of me wanted to push back at him.

"No," I said. "I'm not going anywhere."

He let out another growl, yet nobody from the party heard it.

"Leave," he said, harsher this time. His voice was so powerful that I could almost feel my legs start to move. They *ached* to hurry out of here just because *he* told me so.

"No," I said again, trying to stay in control of my own damn body.

Wrapping a hand around my throat, he buried his face into the crook of my neck and breathed in. His teeth brushed against my skin and made me shiver.

"Is this what you want?" he asked, pushing his hardness against my thigh. "I can't control myself around you tonight. It's the full moon. If you want me to turn you over and *claim* you right here, then stay, Bria. Let me sink my teeth into your neck ..." His teeth pricked the side of my neck.

"Not here," I said in a breathy whisper, glancing back at the party with hundreds of students from my school. "In your office. Please, take me in your office."

Another guttural growl from him made me shiver. He picked me up off the ground, threw me over my shoulder so animalistically, and took long strides toward his office, pushing a key into the lock and stepping into the dark room.

Moonlight flooded into the room through the large window. He set me on his desk, grabbed the front of my dress, and ripped it off me—literally ripped the entire top of it off, as if he really couldn't control himself anymore.

An animal.

Professor Lee was an animal.

He slipped a hand between my thighs, toyed with the bottom of my wet panties, and pushed his fingers inside of them, getting my juices all over him. Just his touch made me clench in excitement. Never in my life had I been touched with such possessiveness, such prowess.

Pushing two of his large fingers inside of me, he rubbed my clit with his thumb, making it swell under his touch. My toes curled, my nipples hardening against the cold air. I threw my head back, feeling the tension rise in my core.

"I've been trying to hold myself back from taking you these past two weeks," Professor Lee growled in my ear, the sound so primal and low, like a monster about to feast on his prey. "Every time you walked in during my office hours, you don't fucking know how much control I had to have to stop myself from bending you over this desk to finally"—he grasped my neck harshly in his free hand, his fingers still driving me wild—"take you."

My toes curled, and I let out a small whimper, letting my fingers curl into his muscular shoulders. "I'm going to come already," I whispered, my body tingling. I was so close—so fucking close.

"You won't come," Professor Lee said to me, forcing me to look up into his glowing golden eyes. "Not unless you ask for permission and not unless I give it to you. Do you understand me, Bria?"

I furrowed my brows, eyes widening slightly, and stared up into those intense eyes.

He roughly rubbed his thumb against my jaw. "Do. You. Understand?"

Though the pressure kept building, I nodded and dug my fingers deeper into his shoulders. "Can I come, Professor Lee?" I asked, clenching on his fingers as he added another.

He moved his thumb faster against my clit. "No."

"Please," I begged. "Please ... I'm so close."

"No."

The more he told me no, the closer and closer I came to coming undone around his fingers. My core was pulsing, my nipples were aching, my neck was burning every time his teeth brushed against it.

"God, Professor Lee ... I can't hold out for much longer."

"You're not going to come, Bria. Not yet."

He pulled his fingers out of me, stuck them into his mouth, and groaned as he sucked off all my juices. I reached between us, stroking his hard cock through his jeans and aching for him to be inside of me.

I was desperate to come, so desperate that I inched my ass to the edge of the desk and tried to grind my wet pussy against his hardness. I needed some kind of friction, something to tip me over the edge. I needed it badly.

Before I knew it, he grabbed my hips, knelt between my thighs, and buried his face between my legs, his scruff tickling my inner thighs. He slapped his hand hard against my clit.

"Are you trying to come, Bria?" he asked, lips grazing against my clit. "Are you trying to get off, even when I told you that you couldn't?"

I bit my lower lip and hesitantly nodded. "Yes," I whispered.

He pressed his lips right over my clit, his tongue flicking against it and making me jerk up in pleasure. "Then, you're going to wait even longer." He started to eat my pussy, his tongue moving so quickly and so savagely around my swollen clit, my juices wetting his stubble.

I wrapped my hand in his hair, my legs trembling. "Please, not any longer. Please, Professor Lee ..."

My pussy clenched over and over and over, waiting for him to stuff something big into it. I needed something inside of me. Now.

He pushed two fingers into my pussy, thrusting them in and out wildly and driving me higher. "Squeeze your nipples. Pleasure your tits as I torture this tight fucking pussy."

Higher and higher ... God, I was about to lose it in a couple moments.

I brushed my fingers against my nipples, sending waves of pleasure through my body. He continued to eat my pussy, his tongue driving me absolutely crazy. He growled against my folds, making my clit vibrate.

"Professor Lee—"

"Alpha," he growled again. "You will address me as Alpha."

"Alpha," I whispered, my pussy tightening even more. "Can I please come?"

"No." He paused for a moment, inhaling deeply, and stood. "Not unless my cock is inside of you and you're fucking begging for me to fill your tight, desperate little hole up with my cum."

I sucked in a breath. "Anything," I said in a breathy whisper, spreading my legs wider and hoping he'd thrust himself inside of me. I could already tell how big he was through his jeans, how tight they were plastered to his legs because his cock had grown inside of them. "Please, Alpha. I've been thinking about this moment since the first day of class."

He pushed down his jeans, pulled out his cock, and slapped it against my pussy. He let some spit drip from his lips to his cock and rubbed it in. Gripping both my thighs in his hands, he pushed himself into me slowly.

I furrowed my brows, staring up at him and moaning. "Oh my God." My toes curled. "Oh my God. Oh my God. Oh my God."

He continued to push inch after inch after inch into my tight pussy until I was full—completely full.

After a few moments, he closed his eyes and groaned. "Fuck, I didn't think you'd feel this good, baby." He pumped himself in and out of me slowly at first. "My mate feels so fucking warm and tight. It's almost as if you haven't been sticking those cute little vibrators up here every night."

My pussy tightened on him. "You ... you know about them?" I asked.

When he reopened his eyes, they were glowing brighter than before, and his canine teeth had lengthened a damn inch. My heart pounded inside my chest, my breath catching in my throat. Why was this turning me on so much?

"How could I not? Listening to those moans of yours. Smelling your wet cunt every class. You even brought one to class last Friday, didn't you? Trying to fucking tease me while I was trying to teach."

"Lee," I whispered, the tension building up even more, "I'm going to come. I can't hold it back anymore. You're driving me insane."

He grasped my chin and pulled me to him, pressing his lips against mine and kissing me so hard yet so passionately. When he pulled away, he breathed as hard as I was. "When I sink my teeth into your neck, you're going to come for me, Bria."

"Sink your teeth into my neck?" I asked, clenching harder.

The tips of his canines pricked against my skin, and suddenly, he sank his teeth into me. Pressure and pain shot through my body, yet something inside me found pleasure in the way he so unapologetically claimed me with his teeth. He sank them deeper and deeper until all I could feel was his saliva rolling down my chest and his warm gums on my neck.

My body trembled in pleasure, nails digging into the wooden desk so hard that it left scratches and deep grooves.

"Alpha," I panted, doubled over and trembling. "Oh my God, Lee." I bucked my hips back one last time and cried out, coming all over his cock.

After a few moments, he pulled his teeth out of me and licked the blood off my neck, forcing the wound to seal closed. He trailed his nose up to my ear, a purr-like sound rumbling from his chest. He buried himself even deeper inside of me and stilled completely. "Bria, you're mine. Say it for me."

"I'm yours," I breathed out, pussy tightening around him.

"Fuck," he whispered, bucking his hips and coming deep inside my pussy.

When he finally pulled back out, I collapsed onto the desk with the mark on my neck burning. He dressed me in a spare change of clothes from his closet, scooped me into his arms, and walked with me out of his office.

"What are you doing?" I asked.

"You're a wolf now, Bria. Your whole life is about to change," he said. "I'm bringing you home to rest before you shift."

Chapter Nineteen

CALLUM

I marked Bria Benton last night.

Staring up at the ceiling with Bria tucked under my arm, I blew out a breath and let reality sink in. I had waited my whole life—for forty-three damn years—to find my mate. Now, she was finally here with me, where she belonged.

But in the next few weeks, Bria would become more animalistic, would grow canines and claws, ache for her belly to be swollen with pups, like all she-wolves did once they found their mates. And, fuck …

Bria shifted in my arms, her head falling back against the pillow over the crook of my elbow and her lips parted slightly. The blankets covered her nearly naked body, but boy, did I want to rip them off of her and take her.

Like all alphas, I wanted pups as soon as possible. I wanted my family lineage to continue. Our sons and daughters would be stronger than Bria and me and would become the greatest leaders of their time. Though … with Adan sitting on the edge of my property and Bria not even have shifted once yet, pups weren't in the foreseeable future.

"It's too early," Bria mumbled, turning over completely and pulling the blankets over her head. "Turn off the light, Jasmine. I'm having a good dream about Professor Lee. Go back to bed."

My lips curled into a small smile, and I shuffled out of the bed and drew the curtains closed. Bria needed all the rest in the world. I didn't even know if she really processed what had happened last night. She nearly fell asleep in my arms on the way back to my pack house.

When she woke up, she'd be in a world full of shock that she was now a werewolf.

That would be the first of many obstacles she'd have to overcome.

After dressing and shutting the door softly behind me, I bumped into Milo, who stood across the hallway with his arms crossed over his chest and his dark brow arched hard.

"Why didn't you tell me that Adan is after your mate? We could've brought her here to protect her."

"I didn't want to draw attention to her," I said, walking down the hall toward my office and keeping my voice quiet. "It's bad enough that one of the most ruthless alphas in New England is after a human girl. If he—or The Council—found out that she was my mate too, they'd work twice as hard to find her."

Milo followed me into my office and collapsed into one of the plush red seats. "Fuck The Council," he growled. "They're getting on my nerves. They're trying to control all the packs on the continent."

"Fucking tell me about it."

If they found out that I had a human mate, they'd be all fucking over her. Even more than Adan was. They were old, traditional sons of bitches who wanted to keep werewolf blood pure. If they knew about Bria, they might even try to kill her.

My stomach twisted into knots. Had I made the right decision, biting Bria last night?

"Alpha," Levi said through the mind link. *"Adan is at the edge of our property with his warriors, demanding to see you. What should I do?"*

I glanced at Milo, who stood almost immediately. We hurried out of the room and down the hall past my bedroom. Bria's sweet scent drifted through my nose, and I tensed. If Adan was here, Bria wasn't safe alone.

"Get to the pack house and guard it with your life. Nobody sets a paw inside," I said to Levi.

"Got it," Levi said a couple moments later.

Once I stepped outside, I shifted into my wolf and sprinted toward the edge of my property, where Adan had been fucking camping out lately. My pack warriors parted a path for me and Milo to walk through to come face-to-face with Adan himself.

"Where is she?" Adan asked once one of my warriors tossed me a pair of pants. Teeth lengthening into canines, he growled at me and stepped forward with aggression. "Where the fuck is Bria? I smell her here. Her scent is all fucking over your property."

I pressed my lips together to keep cool, but all I wanted to do was rip this man's head right off his body. What was his damn obsession with Bria, and why the fuck did he want her so badly? She was mine, and nobody—not even Alpha Adan—would tear her away.

"How do you know what she smells like?" I asked through gritted teeth.

Adan let out a ferocious growl. "Answer my question."

"You answer mine first."

After glaring at me for a few moments, he took another threatening step closer and bared his canines. "I don't care if I have to tear down every inch of this town. I will fucking find her. And when I do, I'm taking her back. She's not yours to fuck around with."

My wolf took complete control. I ripped my claws through his shirt collar and thrust him against a tree, canines lengthening and muscles flexing. "Don't threaten me or Bria. I will rip you into two fucking pieces if you touch a damn hair on her head."

"You kill me, and The Council will take away all your power and your people and claim your land as theirs," Adan threatened.

And he was right.

They would take away all my pack's freedoms. Everything I had dedicated my life to.

"You're working for The Council?" I asked.

"I don't work for anyone, Lee." He shoved me off him and back a few feet. "If I did, I would've taken your fucking pack by now." He walked back to where his pack was gathered and nodded to the woods. "Mark my words, Lee: I'll find her. I don't care how long it takes. We have the university and your pack surrounded. Once she leaves, I'll know it."

When he started back through the woods, I growled, "How do you know Bria?"

He had to be looking for her for a damn reason, and I needed to figure it out now.

Adan called over his shoulder, "If I told you that, you'd hand my ass over to The Council."

Once they disappeared, Milo shifted into his human and pointed through the woods. "Why didn't you kill him? He's threatening to take away our luna and your mate. We should have his head now."

As much as I wanted to kill him right then and there, I couldn't.

I fucking couldn't.

The Council would catch word that my pack wiped out another, that I was protecting a human, that Bria was my mate, and we'd lose more than only a couple of warrior wolves in war. We would lose this pack, our family, our luna, *and* my mate. I couldn't fucking risk it.

Not yet.

Not until ... Bria shifted for the first time and I knew that she could protect herself.

Then, I would fucking rip Adan to shreds and take The Council on.

Chapter Twenty

BRIA

"Fuck," I whispered.

Clutching my pounding head and sitting up in a bed that wasn't mine, I glanced around the enormous room and cursed at myself. I must've gotten so drunk at the party last night that I imagined going home with Professor Lee rather than some fratty senior.

I ripped the blankets off my body and stared at my naked self.

Double fuck.

What did I drink last night to believe that I had actually found out that Professor Lee was a wolf and that I fucking believed that he had sunk his teeth into my neck? I hopped out of bed and paced the room, stumbling a bit but grabbing onto a chestnut dresser for support.

Did I actually lose my virginity to a rando last night? I had wanted it to be Lee so badly.

Black stars danced in my vision, and suddenly, everything appeared so much sharper. After I squeezed my eyes shut to adjust to the change in vision, I reopened them to stare directly into the dresser mirror, and everything returned back to normal.

Except ...

Nothing was normal.

I stood in the middle of a stranger's room, completely naked, with ... a mark on my neck. Four puncture wounds, where I had dreamed Professor Callum Lee had marked me with his canine teeth last night.

My eyes widened.

It wasn't a dream.

After drawing my finger over each of the scars, I stiffened.

Oh my God.

I was now a wolf. A fucking werewolf.

Yesterday, I didn't even think that they existed. And now, my sight was already starting to change. What would be next? Would I grow fur on my human body? Grow a snout? Canines? Claws? God, I hoped that I didn't have to run with a pack, too, because I hated running.

Moving closer to the mirror, I touched every inch of my face to check for any other wounds or differences, but I found nothing. At least, not yet. My stomach twisted into knots. What was going to happen to me? And where had Callum gone? Should I even call him that?

He was still my professor.

Once I found some clothes to wear, I opened his bedroom door and stepped out into a huge hallway, decorated with carved wooden accents. Wandering down the hall, I glanced into a couple of spare bedrooms and scrunched my nose.

Professor Lee lived in a mansion or something. I had never seen this many rooms in one hallway in my entire life, except Adan's house. I had only been there once, but there were so many rooms and so many people that I had gotten lost one too many times.

The last door on the left was open ajar, and I glanced into it, hoping that Lee was inside. Filled with books with tattered spines and shelves that covered almost every wall that wasn't a window, a large and empty library sat inside.

My eyes widened, and I walked in and down the rows of books, drawing my fingers alongside a bookcase until I reached the window. Outside, a group of people, both old and young, chatted together on the lawn—some sunbathing, others barbequing, and the children chasing each other.

A couple of wolves ran up to the group and shifted into humans, their carved bodies bending at all sorts of angles and their bones snapping in and out of place. The shift looked easy and so simple for them, as if they had been doing it for years.

One last wolf approached the ground and shifted. My jaw snapped open when Jasmine stood naked in front of the group, her silky hair flowing in the breeze and her claws shortening into nails.

I cracked the window open, the air thick and heavy here ... or maybe that was my mind making it seem like I was suffocating. A chilly fall breeze blew into the room, and I inhaled sharply. So many different scents drifted through my nostrils. Somehow, someway, it seemed like I could smell every aroma within a mile—something that had never ever happened before. So, I took another deep breath, the sense intensified.

And then I smelled it.

Adan.

He always had a distinct scent, one of pine cones and honeysuckle.

I tensed and scanned the forest for any trace of Adan. How did he find me?

Back home, I made sure to not leave any damn trace of my whereabouts. I even told my parents that I was off to a college fifty miles from here. How could ... how could Adan find me so quickly and so soon?

My stomach twisted into tight knots.

If he knew where I was, then Mom and Dad knew where I was, and that meant ... the others weren't too far behind.

Fuck. I ran my hand through my hair and backed away from the window a few feet. Fuck, fuck, fuck, fuck, fuck. What was I going to do? The others were ... dangerous. If they found me, I didn't doubt that they would put a bullet through Callum's head.

Or worse ...

When I took another step back, I hit a hard chest and jumped into the air, screaming in pure shock. Someone grabbed my arms from behind and pulled me closer, drawing his nose up the side of my neck.

"Bria ..."

Chapter Twenty-One

CALLUM

"What are you doing in here?" I asked Bria.

She whipped her head around, pieces of her hair flying into my face, and blew out a deep breath. "Oh my God, you scared me. I thought ..." After taking another peek outside, she shook her head. "Nothing. I'm just glad it's you."

"Are you okay?" I asked her, eyeing her arm hairs sticking straight up. I grabbed her hand and drew my thumb over the pulse on her wrist, feeling the quickened pace. "You shouldn't be up so soon. Your body needs time to rest."

Bria furrowed her brows, then glanced back out the window at my pack members on the lawn below. When she looked back at me, her eyes were filled with confusion. "Is ... is Jasmine a wolf too? Levi?"

Jasmine and Levi stood together on the lawn, pushing each other and bickering. I didn't know why I asked them both to watch Bria; they could never quite get along, even when they were growing pups.

"Yes."

"And you're the ..."

"The alpha."

After gulping, Bria walked around the library steadily. She was taking this much better than I anticipated. I expected her to deny everything that had happened last night between us, even the mark on her neck.

As if she could feel that I was thinking about it, Bria brushed her fingers against the mark and smiled softly, desperately trying to wipe the grin away before I could see it. But her fingers continued to play with the four large scars on her throat, where my canines had been last night.

"What're you smiling for?" I asked, leaning against the bookcase.

"No reason," Bria said, full-on grinning now.

"You're not angry?"

"Nope."

"Upset?"

"Nope."

"Have questions?"

Bria pulled a book from the bookcase, the book about a myth only passed down through people with wolf blood. She eyed it for a couple moments, then flipped it open and flicked through the pages.

"I already know mostly everything," Bria said with a smirk.

My lips curled up, and I stepped closer to her to trap her between me and the bookcase. I brushed my fingers up the sides of her arms and made her shiver. She tensed and stopped flipping the pages, her breath catching in her throat.

"Is that right?" I asked, drawing my nose up the side of her neck.

"Yes, actually."

I laced a hand into her hair and gently grasped a fistful of it, tugging back. "How's that?"

"You don't want to know," Bria said, excitement in her voice.

"Try me," I murmured against her bare neck, my teeth grazing against her mark.

Fuck, I wanted to give her another one. I wanted to bite her again, harder and deeper and longer. My heart stammered in my chest, and I grabbed her hips from behind and pulled her ass closer to me. Give her a pup right here and right now. Fill her with a thick load.

"Fine." She snapped the book closed and turned around, staring me right in the eyes. She glanced down at my bare chest, drew her tongue across her bottom lip, and looped her finger around my belt loop. "I've been reading werewolf smut."

"Werewolf smut?" I asked, amused, then chuckled. "Where'd you find that?"

"Oh, you know, online," Bria said, moving her hand lower down my jeans and cupping my dick through them with her small hand. "You don't know how many horny women there are on some of those reading apps. You can find some freaky shit."

"Is that right?"

She stroked my dick up and down, then pulled down my zipper. "Yep."

I stiffened, on the brink of losing control again, like I had last night. Bria really wanted to test my patience today. The full moon might've been last night, but now that my mate was marked, this feeling between us only intensified.

"Want me to show you what I read about?" she asked, slipping her hand into my pants.

A growl rumbled through my chest. I inhaled the sweet scent of her cunt sharply and tried my hardest to stay in control, but it was slipping so quickly that I couldn't stop my canines from lengthening.

Bria fell to her knees in front of me, her back pressed against the bookshelf and her face level with my dick. Curling her fingers around the waistband of my pants and underwear, she pulled them to my knees, my cock nearly smacking her in the face when it sprang out.

"I've been waiting forever to do this," she breathed, wrapping her hand around the base and putting her hot little mouth on my head, sucking lightly and staring up at me.

I placed one hand on the bookcase, fingers turning white against the metal, and gently grasped her chin in the other, drawing my thumb across her lower lip. Damn, she looked so fucking sexy with my cock in her mouth like that. But I didn't know how much her tiny throat would be able to take.

With drool already rolling down her chin, she sucked a couple more inches into her mouth, not even taking half of my dick into her, and pulled back, cheeks flushing. After swallowing hard, she sucked me back in, getting another inch deeper.

"Bria," I grunted, staring down into her watering eyes.

She pressed her thighs together and forced another inch in, gagging slightly when I hit the back of her throat. My hand traveled to her hair, and I curled my fingers, pulling her toward me. Nothing could compare to being in her pussy, but this was damn close.

With watering eyes, she pushed herself closer to me, taking the last few inches of my dick and choking on it, yet she didn't pull away. Instead, she wrapped her lips tightly around the base and sucked on it over and over, her throat tightening around me.

"Fuck," I murmured.

When she closed her eyes, I tightened my grip on her hair. "Keep your eyes open. I don't want you to miss a second of this."

She reopened her watery eyes, gagged, and pulled back, spit, slobber, and drool running down her chin and neck. "More." She moved closer to me, taking my cock again inside her hot mouth, and began bobbing her head.

Moving back and forth so quickly, I tightened my grip on the bookcase and nearly bent the metal. "Bria," I warned. "If you keep bobbing your head like that, you're going to make me ..."

She pulled back slightly, strings of spit running from my cock to her mouth. "Come?"

My eyes rolled back in my head, and I clenched my jaw. I was moments from releasing inside of her mouth, but I wanted the rest of my cum deep in her cunt. Every time I came from now on, it would be inside of her.

So, I grabbed her arm, pulled her to her feet, and pushed down the gym shorts she wore of mine to her knees. She yelped out, but she let me pull one of her legs into the air and stuff my cock deep in her wet pussy. She grabbed on to the bookshelf for support, placing her hand over mine.

I grunted when my balls smacked against her entrance, then thrust in and out of her quickly. She tightened around me and threw her head back, eyes glazed over with lust.

"Oh my God, Callum ... I'm going to come."

"Not until I do."

Hiking her leg higher up my arm, I spread her legs further apart and pounded into her pussy. When she began pulsing around me and whimpering into my shoulder, I came inside her tight hole, filling her to the brim with my cum and *hopefully* with my pups too.

Chapter Twenty-Two

BRIA

"Why are we leaving so early?" I asked, walking with Professor Lee in the forest, back toward the university, on Monday morning.

He glanced around almost nervously, spotted his warriors near the trees, and continued forward.

I arched a brow. "And why are you looking around so nervously? If you didn't want anyone to see me with you, you should've let me leave after you."

"Quiet down," Professor Lee said, tugging me closer to him.

From a distance, I spotted university grounds, then Jasmine and Levi waiting for us.

He intertwined his fingers with mine and squeezed. "You're going to stay with them all day."

"Why?"

"Because, Bria."

"But I was with them all weekend, when you were working and *weren't* fucking me."

"Bria," Professor Lee almost scolded.

"Callum."

He rubbed a hand across his face and sighed. "Someone is looking for you. Promise me that you're not going to wander off today. I don't want you getting hurt and taken from me, and I have work to do here. Stay with them, please."

"Who's looking for me?" I asked, my stomach twisting into knots.

"Don't worry about it," Callum said, taking my chin in his hand gently. "I'll handle him, but I have to go. Promise me that you'll stay with Jasmine and Levi today. No roaming after my class."

While I wanted to roll my eyes at him, I gave him a smile and nodded. "Sure."

Thirty minutes later, I sat in Professor Lee's class with Jasmine and Levi by my side, like they had been all weekend, with my stomach in knots because someone was looking for me and with a great need to pee out all the orange juice I had this morning.

Well, that's what I told them I needed to do.

Jasmine insisted that she needed to come with me, but somehow, I convinced her that she didn't and that the school was safe. Really, I needed some time to breathe—alone. This entire weekend, I hadn't been left alone once. And being the introvert that I was, I fucking needed it.

At least a couple moments.

So, I walked toward the bathroom quickly before class started. We had an exam today.

"Bria," someone said from behind me.

My body froze. I knew that voice.

I turned around slowly to see the one and only Adan hurrying toward me. Before I had the chance to respond, Adan grabbed my hand and slipped into the women's bathroom, locking the door.

"What are you doing here?!" I whisper-yelled at him, smacking him on the shoulder and shoving him back. "I told you when I left not to come and find me, and you did just that! You need to leave."

"I can't," Adan said, glancing at the door. He pulled me farther into the bathroom and into the farthest stall from the door, where we could get the most privacy. "Listen, you're in trouble. Your parents—"

"Did you lead them here?"

"No, but they know where you are and they're looking for you to bring you home."

I crossed my arms. "They will never find me—unless *you* bring them to me. I've cut off all communication and have even deleted all my old social media. I'm fine, Adan. I don't need your protection anymore."

Adan grasped my chin tightly. "You *do* need my protection. You don't understand the first fucking thing you're getting yourself into with them. You don't really know who your parents are, Bria Benton."

After shoving him hard, I poked him in the chest. "If you know it all, then tell me. Who are they? Hmm? Because I'm tired of being their fucking toy that they can use whenever they need me. I don't deserve that."

He pressed his lips together and glanced down. "I know you don't."

"Who are they?" I asked, tapping my foot and not having time for these games.

Silence.

"You're still not going to tell me? Not even when I'm in danger, supposedly?"

"If I could tell you, I would."

"No, you wouldn't." I seethed, shoving him back again, so hard that the bathroom stall door swung open and the bottom hinge came off completely. "This is why I left and didn't stay with you. You keep too many secrets."

Adan widened his eyes at the force of my push, then furrowed his brows and sniffed me. That man fucking sniffed me like he used to, his nose in my hair and his eyes glowing the slightest color of gold.

He clenched his jaw and went to push some hair behind my shoulder.

But Callum told me to hide my mark at school because humans lived here too.

So, I stepped back and away from Adan before he could touch me.

"What happened to you?" Adan asked. "What has Callum done?"

I arched a brow. "I don't know what you're talking about, Adan. Lee is my professor."

Adan growled, so faint but the sound resembled the way Callum did in my ear every night this weekend. "His scent is all over you."

"He's my professor."

"I must've not been clear, Bria. Why the fuck is your professor's scent all over you?"

Narrowing my eyes at him, I stepped closer and refused to let him intimidate me. "And how can you smell another man's scent? I haven't even seen him today yet, so stop being jealous. It's never looked good on you, not even while we were—"

Adan let out another ferocious growl. "I have to go. Stay away from Lee. Hell, stay away from everyone in this fucking school. I'll see you tomorrow." He started toward the locked bathroom door.

"No, you won't."

"Yes, Bria." He turned back to me, nostrils flaring and teeth bared. "I will."

"Well, I'm not leaving my dorm room."

"Well then, I'll fucking find your dorm room because we need to fucking talk." Adan furrowed his brows at me in an angry stare, like *I* had done something wrong. "You're in some deep shit, Bria. All I'm trying to do is protect you."

"No, all you're doing is suffocating me."

Adan blew out a breath, shook his head, and stormed out of the bathroom. I glared at the wooden door, my hands clenched into tight fists by my sides, and marched back to the classroom in time for class to start. When I reached the auditorium door, Professor Lee clenched his jaw—again, another man being angry at me for some ungodly reason—and gestured to the front.

"Where did you go?" he asked quietly, voice tense.

"To the bathroom."

"I told you that you're not safe alone," he said.

Jasmine and Levi glanced at each other, and I glared at Lee. It was wrong, and I was taking my anger from Adan out on Professor Lee. But all this weekend, I had felt suffocated from him forcing someone to be at my side at all times. Part of me felt like this back home, and that was one of the many reasons that I moved away.

I had come to college to start over and to be my own damn person.

Yet people still tried to push things on me.

After giving me another hard stare, Callum stood in front of the class and cleared his throat. "Clear your desks and take out a pencil or pen. We have our first exam today."

Aimlessly, I pulled out a pencil and stared at the wooden desk, my mind reeling with thoughts about what Adan had said. He wasn't lying about protecting me from my parents; he had done that for the past four years. I just didn't know what they were up to *this* time.

Professor Lee placed an exam paper on my desk. I stared down at the questions, not really able to comprehend any of them because all I could think about was this weekend, being turned into a wolf, and now Adan and my parents.

I could feel it in the pit of my stomach. Something bad was about to happen.

Chapter Twenty-Three

CALLUM

The exam should've taken everyone at least forty-five minutes.

But Bria stood up thirty minutes into the class with all her answers bubbled in and words scribbled all over her test. She handed me the papers, barely looking me in the eye. I grabbed them from her tightly, wanting to tell her to go sit back down, to look over her answers again.

She might've been good at mythology, but she hadn't seemed focused since she came back from the bathroom. And our mind link hadn't formed yet, so I couldn't hear what was bothering her or tell if it was me who was being overbearing or not.

"Bria," I said quietly when she let go of the paper.

After glancing up at me briefly, she turned on her heel and hurried down the walkway toward the auditorium exit. I balled my other hand into a fist behind my back, loathing the way that she refused my orders to stay with Jasmine and Levi at all times and wanting to run after her, snatch her by the back of the neck, and sit her on the desk in front of me.

But that would be too obvious to the humans here.

When the door closed, my phone buzzed.

Bria: I need some time alone.

Bria: My parents are being assholes.

Bria: I'm going back to my dorm room.

I set the phone down on the auditorium front desk and pressed my lips together, my canines slicing into my bottom lip. All I wanted to do was run after Bria and bring her back here. She shouldn't be out there alone. Who the hell knows—

"Alpha," Beta Milo said through the mind link. *"Adan was spotted, leaving university grounds."*

The desk broke beneath my death grip, the metal snapping and garnering attention from some of the human students. Werewolf students tensed, listening through the mind link.

Jasmine glanced up at me and sucked in a breath, quickly scribbling the last of her answers, and smacked her unfinished test in my hand.

"I'll find her," she said.

Jasmine rushed down the walkway and disappeared through the doors. My heart pounded in my chest, my throat drying. That fucking asshole had the damn audacity to step onto my school grounds, where Bria was roaming freely. She didn't know what was really going on, and I knew that I should've told her.

I fucking knew it.

But this was all new to her. She might've read up on some wolf romance books, but she didn't understand that the killing actually happened. It wasn't a fable or myth. Wolves killed each other and, sometimes, had no remorse for it.

Adan wouldn't care.

My stomach tightened, my wolf about to take over in front of all these people. I blew a deep breath from my nose and waited impatiently for Jasmine to say something, anything, through the mind link because ... fuck.

"She's with me," Jasmine finally fucking said.

My shoulders slumped forward, yet I still had a bit of annoyance that Bria decided to go directly against my wishes. She was putting herself in harm's way, and she knew it. She fucking knew it. I couldn't lose my mate, not after all this time.

* * *

The moment the last student finished his test, I hurried out of the room and toward Bria's dormitory. I had never been inside before, but I didn't care. I needed to get in there to have a little chat with Miss Bria Benton.

After passing the security guard who was in my pack, I pounded my hand against Bria's door. Jasmine pulled the door open, and Bria sat on her bed in her small room and sighed, pulling the blankets over her head.

"Why?"

"We need to talk."

Jasmine excused herself from the room and shut the door behind her.

"I told you not to leave class."

No response.

"Why did you not listen to me?"

No response.

Instead of talking to her, I grabbed the blankets and ripped them off of her. Bria was curled into a ball with tears pouring down her face and her eyes puffy and red. She placed a hand over her mouth and bit back a cry.

"Go away," she whimpered.

My anger dissipated quickly. I stepped closer to her, sat on the edge of her bed, and scooped her into my arms, placing her head on my shoulder and gently rubbing circles on her back. "What's wrong?"

Entire body tensing at the question, she shook her head. "Nothing."

"You're crying. It's obviously not nothing, Bria."

"My parents are being ... stupid." She glared down at the carpeted floor and pressed her lips together. "I hate them so much. I left because they had been nothing but rude to me. And now ... now, they want me to come back."

"You're not going anywhere," I assured.

Nobody would take Bria from me, not even her parents.

"Come on," I said, hopping off the bed and heading for the door. "I'm taking you home."

"No." She jumped out of my hold and wiped the tears from her cheeks with the back of her hand. "I don't want to go. I want to stay here tonight. I've been at your pack all weekend, and I'm so tired."

"Well, you're not staying here and crying all night by yourself."

"I don't want to go."

I gritted my teeth together. "You're coming with me. You're not safe here."

"I'm not safe anywhere!" she shouted, then quickly regained her composure and looked at the ground. "I mean, you haven't left me alone for days. Nobody has. I'm constantly being looked over or watched."

"I'm protecting you."

She crossed her arms. "I'm still not going."

"The hell you're not."

I threw Bria over my shoulder and walked out of the room with her. Bria was mine, and I wouldn't let her sulk here alone.

Chapter Twenty-Four

BRIA

"So, how'd you do on the exam?" Jasmine asked me, sitting on a bench in Callum's backyard in a tank top and a pair of shorts.

Other pack mates sat at tables and on picnic blankets around us, chatting with each other.

I sank deeper into my sweatshirt, unsure how anyone could be warm in this fall wind, and groaned in response.

Adan fucking pissed me off.

Because of him, I failed that test, had a shitty attitude toward Callum earlier, and constantly looked over my shoulder to see if Adan was coming to find me again. If he kept coming around, then Mom and Dad would surely find me. I glanced over at Callum sitting at a table with a couple of his warriors—that was who he told me they were—and frowned.

I wouldn't let Mom and Dad take anyone else away from me.

They had already stolen my life. Now, they wanted more.

All for money.

That was all their daughter was worth, apparently.

"That bad, huh?" Levi asked, arching a thick brown brow. "You can always suck off your mate to get a better—"

Jasmine elbowed Levi so hard in the ribs that they cracked. I winced and scrunched my nose as Levi doubled over the table and grasped his side, giving Jasmine a side-eye.

"All you have to do is tell me to shut up, not break my bones."

"I've tried that approach before with you," Jasmine said. "And it doesn't work."

Rolling his eyes, Levi turned back to me. "As I was saying ..."

My lips curled into a small smile, and I suppressed a giggle. Man, this guy never learned his lesson, not even after having his ribs broken.

So, I leaned forward toward Jasmine. "If he says any more shit, go for his spine next time."

"Goddess-damn ..." Levi said, smacking his lips shut. "She-wolves are ruthless."

"In a couple weeks, I won't be the one breaking your bones, Levi," Jasmine said, taking a bite of her burger. "Bria will snap you into two pieces, chew you up, spit you out, and leave you for the rogues if you talk back to her."

Levi leaned closer to me and smirked, as if he was challenging me. "I don't think so."

From across the yard, Callum growled so lowly that I ... clenched. Levi quickly moved back into his seat and picked up his burger, his entire body now tense, his head bowed, and his gaze connected with his plate.

My breath caught in my throat at how quickly a growl from Callum could put anyone in their place. Anyone, except me, of course.

I might've hated how jealousy looked on Adan, but on Callum ...

Whew!

All I had to say was that I loved it more than I should've. Jealous, overly possessive, even over the top suited Callum Lee, my Classics professor and now ... my boyfriend, if I could even call him that.

So much so that I wanted to make him even more possessive of me.

And I knew just the way—for tomorrow in class.

Jasmine smiled. "If you haven't noticed, alphas are extremely possessive of what's theirs. Alpha Lee has already told Levi to stay away from you, and someone"—she turned her glare to Levi—"can't listen to *any* orders ever."

Levi straightened his back. "I don't listen to or—"

Lee growled again, and Levi snapped his mouth shut. I suppressed a giggle and finished the rest of my food. Callum glanced over at me, as if he wanted to come over and talk, but I turned away, still sorta, kinda angry at myself for getting pissed at him today *and* failing his test. Besides, I didn't like the attention on me when I was with him, not yet anyway.

I didn't know any of his pack mates, and they all seemed very talkative and loud and close while I was quiet Bria Benton, who was trying to get over her confidence issues and running away from a family that had never accepted her.

Uneasiness settled over me. I stood, politely excused myself from dinner, and tossed my plate in the trash, my social battery suddenly drained. Slipping through the back pack house door, I ran up a flight of stairs to the library and shut the doors behind me, breathing in the calming scent of ancient paper and decade-old books.

After pulling a random book from the shelf, I settled down into one of the library chairs and flipped it open, a drawing of a wolf on the first page, accompanied by the title *One Alpha*. I arched a brow and turned the page, glancing through the summary to see if it was something I'd enjoy reading.

"Ooh! Great choice!" an older woman said, walking over to me from an aisle in the library. Striking silver hair that came to her mid-back and piercing brown eyes, she gestured to the book. "Has Callum taught you about the One Alpha myth yet?"

I glanced back down at the book, then at her. "Not yet."

"Oh Goddess, that's more surprising than finding out he has a human mate," the woman said, giving me a small smile. "Callum loved this book when he was a boy. I secretly think that's what turned him into a mythology-obsessed professor."

Not knowing what to say, I shifted in the seat, placed the book in my lap, and smiled. What could I even say to her? I didn't know her at all; Callum hadn't really introduced me to anyone this weekend, had basically locked us both away in his pack house for days.

"You're Bria, right?" she finally said.

My lips curled into a soft smile. "Yes."

She sat in the chair beside me and placed a hand on my knee. "I'm Callum's mom."

Cheeks flushing, I sat up taller and grasped the book until my knuckles turned white. "Oh, sorry, I didn't know! I'm Bria," I said stupidly after she literally just said my name, embarrassing myself even further. I nervously rubbed my sweaty palm on my jeans. "Sorry. I, um ..."

"Don't worry about it, sweetheart." Callum's mom gently patted my knee. "Anyway, I wanted to introduce myself to you since Callum has been keeping you to himself, like I expected him to. I'll let you get back to that book." She glanced down at it once more. "You'll enjoy it."

Once she left, I glanced out the library window at Callum outside, easily chatting with his pack. I hugged *One Alpha* to my chest and frowned. I could barely chat with his mom without making an ass of myself.

Being a luna was going to be more incredibly difficult than anything else.

Maybe even more difficult than dealing with The Council.

Chapter Twenty-Five

CALLUM

Bria walked into class on Wednesday with the exam that she got a seventy percent on crumpled up in one hand and her brows furrowed together in an annoyed glare. After I handed it to her yesterday, she barely talked to me after class. I had to fuck her pissed expression right off her face last night, but now, it was back.

But Bria had to learn one way or another. I wouldn't go easy on her because she was my mate. Memorizing and learning classics might've been difficult for some people, but Bria had to know it. She was my mate, and some of these stories weren't fables. They were real history.

Sitting down in her usual seat, she crossed her arms and stared at me with those full pink lips pressed together. While Bria was usually a straight-A, good-girl student, today, she took out her phone, placed it on her desk, and tapped open an app, all the while giving me a dirty look, as if she wanted to test me after everything that happened this past weekend.

Suddenly, I heard a small vibration start and watched her tense slightly. I pressed my lips together, knowing that every other wolf in this room could probably hear the sound of a vibrator stuffed up my mate's cunt.

"Bria," I said through gritted teeth two minutes before class started. "Up here. Now."

Bria stood and readjusted her dress, walking rather funnily up to my desk. I snatched her by the elbow and dragged her to the corner of the room, jaw twitching.

"What the fuck are you doing in class with that?" I asked through gritted teeth, referring to the vibrator between her legs, humming so softly but intensely enough to make her cunt soaked already. I could fucking smell it.

"Making sure that you take your own advice," she said, shoving her exam toward me.

"Take my own advice?" I asked, about a second away from pulling that vibrator out of her, locking her away in my office, and having my way with her later.

She crossed her arms, pointed to my note that I left on her exam, and smirked. "*Pay attention in class*, Professor Lee." She leaned closer to me, her tongue gliding across her full pink lips. "To me."

And with that, she sauntered back to the front row and sat, her legs spread ever so slightly and her navy-blue dress moving up her pale thighs. I swallowed hard, knowing that I had to keep my eyes off her or I would lose control right in the middle of class around some of these other humans.

Walking around, writing on the whiteboard, teaching students about my favorite classics, I caught sight of Bria, spreading her legs a bit wider for me to see. I tried to pull my gaze away, tried so fucking desperately, but ... I couldn't.

Our mind link connection might've only been forming, but I could hear the beginning of her thoughts, how she wanted to see my wolf again, my claws, my canines, my cock burrowed into her tight cunt.

Pants tight around my growing cock, I grabbed some papers

from the desk—as if I were looking them over—then held them in front of me, so nobody would see how hard I was for Bria already. She fucking did something to me that no other woman had been able to before.

Bria stared right at me and pushed some hair behind her shoulder, showing me the four large canine scars that I had given her last Friday night. She brushed her fingers over them, gripped on to the desk, and pressed her trembling thighs together, brows furrowed together the way they did right before she came.

"Class is dismissed early today," I said, taking raspy breaths and clutching the papers so hard that my claws dug right through them. "Be ready to dive in to horror classics on Friday."

Everyone, including Bria, packed up and headed for the exits. Some wolves from my pack walked up to me with their books to their chests.

"Leave," I growled at them, my canines extended. I couldn't fucking think straight right now and didn't have time to deal with anyone other than my mate, who was quickly walking to the exit.

As they scurried out through a side door, I stormed down the center aisle toward Bria and her pretty little salivating cunt. She opened the door, but I slammed it closed with my palm and grabbed the back of her neck.

"You're not going anywhere."

She tensed and stared up at me, her mind reeling with excitement. "I'm going home."

"You wanted me to pay attention to you, Bria." I locked the entrance to the auditorium and grabbed her hand, placing it right over my hard cock through my pants. "You have my full attention now."

Gasping softly, she chewed on the inside of her lip and curled her fingers around it. "Are you going to ... to bite me again?" she whispered, brushing her other fingers across my mark on her neck and shivering.

"I'll bite you all over your body if you want me to," I murmured into her ear, stepping closer and burying my face in the bare side of her neck.

"And you-your wolf ..."

"What about him, Bria?" I hummed, curling a strand of her dirty-blonde hair around my finger and tugging on it. "He hasn't let me stop thinking about you since Friday, has made me jerk off more times than I can count these past few days, thinking about you. Is that what you want to hear?" I dipped my hand between her legs and touched her cunt through her dress. "Why don't you turn that vibrator of yours back on for me? I want to watch your pussy become a soppy, aching, swollen mess."

Bria sucked in a breath, her cheeks flushed. "Professor Lee—"

I grabbed her jaw and forced her to look up at me. "Alpha."

"Alpha," she repeated, pressing her thighs together. She drew a finger down my hard cock and glanced around the empty auditorium. "I don't think that we should do it here."

Lips curling into a smile, I chuckled and stroked my thumb against her jaw. "Did you think that was a suggestion, Bria? It was an order." I sucked her bottom lip into my mouth and tugged on it gently between my teeth. "Start the vibrator."

Scrambling, she pulled her phone from her pocket, opened an app, and pressed a pink button, the light humming from the vibrator filling the room.

"Do you know why I had to end class?" I asked her, capturing her nipples between my fingers and tugging lightly on them.

She stared up at me with furrowed brows and nails digging into my shoulders and shook her head. I tugged on her nipples harder.

"Because every other wolf in this auditorium could hear these small little vibrations. And nobody hears my mate come, except for me."

She sucked in another breath, cheeks flushing even redder, and swallowed hard.

"How long did it take you to come up with this cute little punishment for me?" I asked her, drawing a finger down the vibrator fastened on her underwear. "Wearing a vibrator in class and wanting all my attention? Hmm?"

"I ... um ..." She pressed her thighs together, as if the vibrations were too much. "A bit ..."

"Give me a number," I said. "Any number."

She shifted from foot to foot and whimpered. "I don't know ... a couple of hours."

My lips curled into a smirk against her skin. "A couple of hours?" I asked, running my hands all over her body. All I wanted to do was take her right here, right now, bend her over one of these chairs and fuck her until she couldn't walk.

It was all I had been thinking about for the past three days. And if anyone caught us, they'd throw us both out of the university.

"I'll have to play with you for a couple of hours, Bria, and not give myself to you because I know you so desperately want it."

She whined again, grasping my hand as I slipped it between her legs again to rub that swollen cunt.

"You don't have to play with yourself to get my attention, but ..." I pressed my cock against her stomach to let her feel how hard I was for her. "It does make me ready to take you anytime, anywhere. It's too bad that I can't give it to you today, Bria." I undid my belt and pushed her hand into my pants to let her feel me. "Only good girls get it." I trailed my nose up the side of her neck and captured her earlobe between my teeth. "And you've been bad."

"Please, Prof—" she started, fingers curling around my cock. "Please, Alpha."

Unable to stop myself, I growled into her ear at the sound of my little human mate calling me her alpha. I pulled her off the door and leaned her against the back of one of the many auditorium chairs, pushing her legs apart and kneeling between them. Before I could stop myself, I yanked her underwear to the side and pressed my mouth to her warm clit.

"Alpha L-Lee ..." She moaned, thrusting a hand into my thick hair and pulling my face closer to her cunt.

I drew my tongue across it, licking and lapping up her juices, my wolf quickly taking control of me and eating his mate's wet pussy like it was his first taste.

She leaned back, legs trembling and brows furrowed together. "I-I want you to feel good too," she murmured, moaning softly again. "Please, let me have it. I know that you want to fill me again. I know how much you loved it last time. Take me, Alpha, please."

I pressed a hand against my pants and stroked myself through my pants. I couldn't let her have it, not until she learned not to come into my classroom and touch herself. That was my job. So, I buried my face deeper between her legs and flicked my tongue across her clit, making her scream out.

"P-p-please," she pleaded.

Pushing two fingers into her pussy, I stood between her legs and pulled down my pants enough for my cock to spring out and smack against her pussy. Breathing hard, she gripped on to my shoulders and stared down at the head of my cock pressing against her hole. I rubbed it against her entrance, getting it wet.

"Do you want it, Bria?" I asked, wanting nothing more than to feel her grip on to me as I thrust into her. When she nodded at me, I cracked a smirk. "Beg for it then. I want to hear you begging for your alpha's cock to be buried inside of you."

With her legs trembling even harder, I rubbed the head of my cock against her clit, back and forth and back and forth, feeling myself tighten.

She threw her head back, toes curling. "God, please, give it to me ... please. I can't ..." She parted her lips, eyes wide. "I ... I'm ... I'm going to—"

"Come for me, Bria," I whispered, holding myself back. "You'll get my cock later when you show me how much of a good girl that you can be."

Bria pulled her knees together and slapped a hand over her mouth, moaning loudly into it, and came.

Chapter Twenty-Six

BRIA

"Did you seriously bring me back to your pack house, so I could study?" I asked Callum as he walked into his office.

Before he could see me *not studying*, I hid the *One Alpha* mythology book that Callum's mom recommended to me underneath a textbook. I had been sitting at his grand oak desk with a textbook opened to some classics chapter for the past forty-five minutes and hating that I let him touch me so intimately at school.

Okay, I actually loved it, but still.

In the beginning of class, I had all his attention and complete control over him. Five minutes later, he had dismissed class and made my cunt a wet mess only with a couple fingers and his filthy mouth.

But that didn't make this any better. I knew all those questions on his test and got them wrong because of fucking Adan. He fucked with my mind and made me unable to think straight the other day. If Lee had let me redo the test a couple hours later, I would've gotten them all right. I knew I would've.

With his sleeves rolled up his muscular forearms and dark eyes fixed on me, he walked toward me and around his desk, placing a hand on the back of my chair and leaning forward to speak in my ear. "You need to learn, Bria. This is important."

"What about this is im—"

He placed his large, callous hands on my tense shoulders, causing me to immediately suck in a breath. "You'll get a reward every time you answer one of my questions correctly. Sound good?"

"A reward?" I whispered, warmth gathering in my core. "This will ... help me learn?"

"You'll do more than learn." He chuckled darkly in my ear, and then he trailed his fingers up and down the sides of my arms. "Question one: what were the three themes of *The Iliad* that we discussed in class?"

I sucked in a breath, remembering how lost I had been in that class. These past few days, Callum had noticed how unfocused I had been and had somehow made it even more incredibly difficult for me to pay attention to anything that wasn't him. Even during movie clips he showed us, all I could focus on was that chiseled jaw, those plump lips, his—

"An answer, Bria?" he asked, voice husky.

"Revenge. Honor. And ..." I gnawed on the inside of my lips, this an entire guess. "War?"

He trailed his fingers from my arms down to my chest, cupping my breasts over my dress and capturing my nipples between his fingers. "Good girl."

Warmth gathered in my core, my breath catching at the nickname. I adjusted myself in the seat and pressed my thighs together, letting him tug harder and harder on my nipples.

"Are you sure this will help? I-it seems distracting, Professor Lee."

"*Alpha* Lee," he corrected, pulling on my nipples even harder until I cried out.

Wanting to piss him off—just a smidgen—I hummed and waited for my next chance to *not* call him alpha, as he wanted me to. I wanted my control back from earlier, the control he easily commanded from me. It was the only time I could seem to focus on anything other than Adan, my parents, and The Council.

"Question two: when thrown out of their home, who raised Romulus and Remus—"

"A shepherd, *Professor* Lee," I answered before he could finish.

He growled in my ear, making my pussy clench, then pulled his fingers away from my breasts, refusing to even touch them until I answered him correctly. "*Before* the shepherd found them."

My nipples ached, and I so desperately wanted his callous hands all over every inch of my body. I didn't just want his breath on my neck, but I wanted his teeth there as well, sucking on my flesh and making me shiver.

"Before the shepherd found them, they were raised by ruthless, savage, ferocious beasts that let them suckle on their breasts, *Professor.*"

Growling again, Lee grabbed a fistful of my hair and pulled the seat right out from underneath me, shoving me against the desk and pressing his hard cock against my backside. "You want to be smart with me, Bria?"

"Yes," I breathed out, arching my back ever so slightly and rubbing against him. "I do."

He snaked a hand around the front of my throat and pulled me closer. "Answer me correctly this time or else this reward"—he ground himself closer to me, ruining my panties—"goes away for the rest of the fucking night. Do I make myself clear?"

Too horny to refuse it, I bit back a smart-ass answer and whispered, "A wolf. The future founder of Rome and his brother were raised by a she-wolf, according to the mythology."

"Good." Callum relaxed behind me and smirked against my neck, inhaling deeply, then slid his large hand up my thigh until he reached my panties. He hooked his finger around the band, shoved them down to my knees, and fondled my pussy. "You're still so wet for me, Bria. I've been aching to taste this cunt again."

"B-but you …" I breathed out. "Don't you want me to give you a—"

"Not now," he said into my ear, pulling out his fingers and shoving them into his mouth, groaning. "I love watching the faces you make when I'm between your legs …" After he sucked off my juices, he pushed his fingers back inside of me. "Making this little pussy clench." He curled his fingers over and over at the right angle, hitting my G-spot and making me moan. "And these small little moans of yours make you sound like a kitten, Bria. It gives my wolf so much more pleasure than you'd think it would."

My toes curled at the mention of his wolf, that whole other side of him that I had only seen glimpses of before, those golden eyes and sharp canines, ragged breaths and his dominating possessiveness.

"Question three: what do scholars refer to that wolf as?" he continued, stroking my G-spot.

I reached behind me and unzipped his pants, needing to feel his thick, veiny cock in my hand and making him grunt. I moaned at the tips of his teeth gliding across my neck. "Lupa. They called her lupa. *Lupus* in Latin."

"Bria is learning," Professor Lee praised, pulling his fingers from my pussy and rubbing the head of his cock against me to get it wet.

Every time he pushed himself closer, I sucked in a breath and waited for him to push it inside of me, but it never came. He stood behind me, one hand around my neck and his other on my hip, teasing and taunting me with his cock.

"Please, Alpha Lee," I pleaded. "Give it to me. I need it so bad. I have done nothing but imagine it inside of me since last night."

"Patience. Last question," Lee murmured into my ear, his cock pressing against my hole and ready to slide into me at any moment. He trailed his nose up the column of my neck and gently grazed his canine teeth across my soft spot. "Are you ready for it?"

Fingers paling on the classics book pages, I arched my back. "Yes."

"Who do you belong to?"

"You, Alpha."

"That's correct, Bria," he growled against me, the tips of his canines dragging across my skin and making me shiver in delight.

I arched my back and moaned out loud, everything inside of me begging for more and more and more of him.

He wrapped his hand around my chin and forced my head to the side. "Are you ready for your reward?"

Trembling under him, I nodded. "Yes, please."

Professor Lee shoved himself into me ruthlessly and brutishly. Mouth sucking on the soft spot on my neck, he grunted against me and thrust into me over and over and over again. I arched my back and whimpered out, the pleasure rushing through me almost unbearable.

Chapter Twenty-Seven

CALLUM

When I pulled out of Bria, she collapsed on my desk, her swollen lips parted slightly and her eyes glazed over with lust. Some of her textbooks shifted on the desk, revealing my favorite mythology book as a kid.

One Alpha.

I pulled the book from the table and sat back on my chair, tugging Bria into my lap. Bria sat on one of my legs and rested her head on my shoulder, her raspy little breaths coming out quickly. After a few moments, she widened her eyes and stared at the book.

"Oh, ha-ha. I totally *wasn't* reading this while studying," she stuttered.

"Where did you find this?" I asked.

Bria might've thought that I was angry she was reading this instead of her textbook, but part of me felt ... pleased with her. Even if she didn't get an A on the test, Bria was trying to learn more about my culture. She had barely officially met the pack yet, but she wanted to know more.

"Your mom said that you loved this book as a kid," she said.

"My mom? When did you meet her?"

Bria smiled softly. "The other day in the library while you all were eating outside." She pulled her dress down to cover all her bare parts, curled into the crook of my arm, and rested her head on my shoulder. "Tell me what it's about. I'm sure that you're dying to tell me."

And honestly, I had been.

"It's a myth passed down from werewolf to pup throughout the years." I flipped the book open and moved my fingers alongside the wolf drawn on the first page. I had touched this wolf so many times over the years that the page was thinning. "Nobody else knows about it, except us. It's what made me interested in mythology. Mythology might be fiction, but there is an inherent truth to it, which is why it's so important for you to learn the material in class."

"That's why you punished me?" Bria asked, a lightness in her voice.

"For good reason," I said. "Gods and monsters mirror humans in the way they interact. They act, speak, and talk like us. Wolves believe in the Moon Goddess; they worship her even though we've never once seen her face. We believe in her stories, especially this one."

"I've read some of it," Bria said, moving her fingers alongside the wolf, just as I had.

My lips curled into a smile. "I made my mom read this to me every night since I was three until I could read it myself. If she didn't, I'd throw a fit."

"You must've been a pup from hell." Bria giggled. "I mean ... you still kinda are ..."

After arching a brow at her, I found myself chuckling along with her, loving the sound of her laugh. It was hard to believe that I finally found my mate. After waiting decades for her, I had completely dedicated my life to my pack and decided that I wasn't going to find my mate.

But now ... I cherished every moment with her. Even small ones like this.

Because if The Council found out, they could take her from me.

"*One Alpha* has a bunch of stories about our past and our Goddess, the most popular one being about a single alpha centuries ago, who had come to rule all the alphas. He was the strongest of all warriors and led with nothing but goodness in his heart."

"Why is it still popular among the pack?" she asked. "I've seen some people read it in secrecy."

"The book was banned about ten years ago by people who think that he'll be back to control everyone and everything again."

"What do you think?"

"Honestly? As much as I love mythology and wish it *all* to be real, I think that the *One Alpha* is mostly a fable to motivate alphas to lead without violence, so their packs will prosper. Unlike some other myths, there isn't much historical evidence that leads scholars to believe that it's true. But, like most other alphas, I try to be like him sometimes because there is too much bad shit in this world now."

Bria's smile faltered, lips trembling slightly. "I know that all too well ..."

"What happened in your past?" I asked her, shutting the book. "With your parents."

As much as I claimed to lead with compassion, that didn't mean I didn't want to rip someone's head off for hurting my mate, whether that be now or in the past. From what it seemed, Bria's parents hurt her in some way. And I wanted to make it right.

Any way that I could.

"I don't want to talk about it." She shook her head. "Not now."

"Alpha," Milo said through the mind link.

I placed my hand on Bria's knee and growled quietly, pissed that Milo needed me while I was spending time with my mate.

"What is it?" I asked.

"Adan is demanding to see Bria. He knows that she's here."

Fuck.

"I have to go," I said quickly, picking Bria up, placing her on the chair in my place, and kissing her forehead. "Stay here and don't leave, no matter what you hear outside. Do you understand me?"

"What's happening?"

"Nothing, Bria. Someone is just at my pack borders."

Without me having to say anything, Bria stood up, hurried to the window, and inhaled sharply. "Oh no. No. No. No. No. No. I told him to stay away. What the hell is he doing here?" She paced the room, dragging her hands through her hair. "Fuck."

"Bria—"

"Don't hurt him," Bria said quickly, turning toward me. "Please."

"You're in danger. I will do whatever I need to do to protect you."

"Not Adan, please. You can't kill him."

I froze. How the hell did she know who Adan was?

"How do you know Adan?" I asked.

She gnawed on the inside of her cheek and looked down at her feet, sucking in a sharp breath.

I moved closer to her and snatched her chin. "How do you know him? He's dangerous."

"I know he is." She turned away from me. "I've seen him kill before."

"Then, how do you know him? What were you doing with him?"

"Don't get mad at me," she said. After blowing out a breath, Bria finally turned toward me and frowned. "He is my ex-boyfriend, and he's saved me from more than you will ever believe."

Chapter Twenty-Eight

BRIA

"I'm going to kill him," Callum said between clenched teeth, his canines extending and his eyes glowing a bright, piercing gold. He stormed out of his office and down the hallway, heading for the front door. "Rip him to fucking pieces."

I hurried after him. "You promised that you wouldn't get mad."

"I promised that I wouldn't get mad at *you*, Bria." He rushed through the woods, twigs snapping under his harsh footsteps. "I can feel however the fuck I want to feel about the man trying to take my mate away from me."

Oh God. Oh God, oh God.

Moving my short legs faster, I desperately tried to keep up with his quickening pace. This was not how I expected Callum to react. Sure, I had seen him angry and annoyed before, but I had never seen him like ... this.

About half a mile ahead, wolves gathered in a clearing in their shifted forms. My heart pounded inside my chest, and I moved even faster somehow, letting my legs carry me the rest of the way. Callum was about to flip out on Adan, and I didn't want him to get hurt.

If Adan thought he was a threat, he would murder Callum.

Adan was so insane that he smiled when he killed someone.

"Levi," Callum shouted.

A wolf glanced back from the crowd and toward us, and then Levi shifted into his naked human form.

Callum grabbed my hand and pulled me toward Levi. "Bring Bria back to the pack house and don't let her leave."

When he released my hand, he turned toward the crowd and shifted into his huge black wolf, his claws digging into the dirt and his canines dripping with saliva. I stared at him with wide eyes and watched him march right through the crowd of parted wolves.

Before Levi could grab my hand to force me back toward the pack house, I stormed toward the group.

Levi snatched my hips and flung me over his sweaty shoulder. "You're not going over there."

I squirmed in his hold and stared with wide eyes as Callum leaped at Adan—two wolves about to fight to the death. My heart thrashed even harder, and I punched and kicked Levi as hard as I could until I heard one of his bones crack.

And while I wanted to care, all I could seem to focus on was the thought of Adan killing Callum. No matter what, I couldn't let Callum die. He was my mate, the man who turned me into a wolf only a couple of days ago. If he died because of Adan, I would never be able to forgive him.

Never.

I would kill Adan myself, no matter how long it took or how hard it was.

Levi cursed under his breath and scolded me to stop squirming around, but I continued even harder, knowing that I would break him soon. From across the forest, Callum and Adan tore out each other's flesh, growled and bit and ripped each other to pieces, flesh and fur flying in every direction.

"Stop it!" I shouted, but neither of them seemed to hear me.

Adan ripped a huge chunk of Callum's shoulder muscle from his body and was about to tear his claws into Callum's throat. Fear ran through my body, the thought of losing Callum making me numb. I couldn't.

I barely knew him yet, but ...

But I ...

"We love him," someone whispered inside my mind.

I didn't know who it was or how they got inside my head, but it was true. Something had drawn me to Callum the moment that I laid my eyes on him in the hallway. I could barely make eye contact with him; my mind had been in overdrive the moment I smelled his scent the first day of school.

Suddenly, I was running through the forest.

"Bria! Get back here!" Levi screamed from the forest floor.

My eyes widened slightly as I glanced over my shoulder at Levi, who was doubled over on the ground, clutching his stomach with one arm and his shoulder with the other to hold back the gushing blood. I didn't know how the hell that had happened, but ... I'd deal with that later.

"Bria!" Levi shouted, stumbling to his feet. "Stop!"

I turned toward the crowd of wolves fighting each other, my legs moving on their own. Glancing down at them, I noticed the blood on my hands and the claws that had ripped out of my fingers.

Had I ... had I been the one to hurt Levi? Had I taken him down and gotten out of his hold without even my knowledge of it?

Unable to stop myself, I pushed further into the crowd of wolves until I reached the two biggest wolves slashing each other with their talons. Adan swiped his claws across Callum's neck. My chest rose and fell quickly, agony rushing through me.

"No!" I shouted.

But a moment passed, and Callum was still fighting. No blood seeped out of his throat, only a thin scar formed, as if Adan had barely grazed Callum. Maybe Adan wasn't as strong as I had always thought he was, or maybe Callum was stronger.

So much stronger.

Callum rushed at Adan faster this time, pouncing on Adan's body and thrusting him to the ground, blood dripping from Callum's canines and onto Adan's face. Callum roared at Adan, Adan's fur rushing back from the mere force of the growl.

A wolf, who I recognized as Jasmine by the piercing eyes, ran by and slammed Callum in the side, shoving him off Adan. My eyes widened slightly as the scene unfolded around me. What was she doing?

Jasmine stood in front of Adan, as if she was protecting him from her alpha. Instead of taking the gesture lightly, Adan stood back up and growled at Jasmine, pushing her behind him, but his eyes were lighter and livelier than I had ever seen them.

Adan and Callum leaped at each other again, and I couldn't take another second of watching them try to kill the other.

I rushed between them, found myself moving without the ability to stop, and screamed at the top of my lungs, "Stop!"

A deafening silence erupted across the forest, and everyone stopped.

"Bria," Levi said after a couple moments.

"What?!" I snapped at him, my chest heaving up and down. "I'm not coming with you!"

"No, Bria ..." He gestured down at the alphas by my side.

My hands were wrapped around their throats so hard, fingers digging into their flesh until they nearly turned white. My eyes widened, and I let go of them, backing up slowly with my brows furrowed together.

"I ..." I whispered, glancing down at my trembling hands and at the newly found strength that I possessed. "I'm so sorry."

Chapter Twenty-Nine

CALLUM

Bria nervously backed away from Adan and me, her eyes wide in fear. I shifted into my human and coughed up some blood, desperately trying to catch my breath after Bria had nearly choked me to death. Adan shifted beside me, and while I still wanted to rip him to pieces, I couldn't do it when Bria stood mere feet beside me.

I wouldn't put her in more danger. I had ordered Levi to take care of her.

Once I caught my breath, I glanced over my shoulder at Levi, who was doubled over and held an open wound in his shoulder that he hadn't been able to heal yet. I clenched my jaw and cut my gaze to Adan, then stood and grabbed Bria to place her behind me.

"Callum …" she whispered, her hands trembling. "Is that supposed to happen?"

"You're turning into a wolf, Bria," I said, careful not to raise my voice at her.

She might've almost choked me and Adan out, but Bria was still so innocent, still so fragile. She didn't know the first thing about how her body was going to transform. And while I thought I knew how a human body would change, I didn't think she'd become that strong this quickly.

"I knew that you marked her," Adan said, clenching his teeth and holding his wound together, blood rushing through his fingers. He looked over at her. "Why didn't you tell me the other day?"

Bria stood behind me, staring at the blood on her hands, and swallowed hard. "Because I didn't want you to hurt Callum."

I seethed at him, pissed the fuck off that Bria met with Adan and didn't tell me. I fucking knew that something smelled off about her when she came back to my classroom after using the restroom the other day. Goddess, I should've found him and ripped him into two pieces then.

"Why the fuck are you here?" I growled, baring my teeth at him again. "Bria is mine. I don't care what kind of history you have with her. She's *mine* now, and I will fucking kill you if you think otherwise." The words tumbled out of my mouth before I could stop them.

Days ago, I had told Bria that I tried to lead like the One Alpha, without hurting or killing other wolves, without fear from my people. But the mere thought of losing Bria ... drove me crazy.

I would slaughter anyone who got in my way of finally having a mate.

Screw being good for her. I'd kill for her.

"What happened between you and her?" Jasmine asked Adan suddenly.

"Why'd you get in the middle of us?" I asked her, directing my attention toward her and feeling nothing but betrayal from my own packmate. "I was about to kill him, and you fucking stopped me, Jasmine."

Adan stood up and spat some blood at his feet. "Don't fucking talk to her like that."

The anger rushing through me was quickly replaced with shock. "You're mates," I said. It wasn't a question, but a statement.

Jasmine and Adan were mates, and I didn't know how fucking long Jasmine knew about it without saying anything to me.

"Yes," she said, staring at me, then at her feet.

"How long have you been putting your luna in danger for this asshole?" I growled, gesturing to Adan and posturing.

Jasmine sucked in a breath. "Just today, Alpha. I would never allow anyone to hurt Bria. If I had known that he was my mate before, I would've told you. I promise I would have. This pack means everything to me."

Adan grabbed Jasmine's hand and pulled her back behind him. "Get away from him."

"Why are you here?" I asked again, turning my attention to him.

Adan glanced at Bria, and Bria looked back nervously, chewing on the inside of her cheek. His angry expression faltered for a moment, pain clouding his eyes. A part of him either still loved Bria or ... something terrible happened between them.

"What happened?" I asked again, hating being ignored.

Bria gently touched my shoulder. "Callum ..."

Adan stepped forward. "Don't, Bria. The more people who know about it, the easier it will be for them to find you. And if they find you, you know what's going to happen ..."

Bria furrowed her brows and wrapped her arm around mine, leaning closer to me, as if she needed the support. Pain shot through my body, and I knew that it wasn't mine, but Bria's. Whatever happened to Bria before she came to college must've been worse than I thought.

"I'm his mate," she whispered, the words bringing me joy and pride.

No matter what happened between him and her, she was mine. Even she knew it.

"Bria," Adan scolded.

Suddenly, she stepped in front of me and let go, glaring at him. "I told you that I don't need your help anymore. So, stop it, Adan! I can handle it myself. You've done enough already with my brother. You don't need to—"

He stepped closer to her. "The Council will find you and kill you!" Adan growled, eyes glowing gold and canines lengthening again.

My eyes widened. "The Council?"

Bria tensed, her hands balled into fists by her sides.

"You can't protect yourself, no matter how much you think you can!" Adan took another step closer to her and glared down at my mate. "Even I can't defeat The Council alone. They're too powerful for even an alpha to take down. You would be stupid to think you can do it yourself."

"I don't plan to take them down. My plan was to hide, which you've completely ruined!"

Adan ran a hand through his hair, let out a long sigh, and turned around. "You don't fucking get it. No matter how hard you hide, they'll find you. You will never be safe from them. Nobody, not even your mate, will be able to protect you."

I stared at them, bickering back and forth, and tried to piece it all together. Nothing about this made any sense. Why would The Wolf Council be after Bria? Why were they looking for her? And most importantly, why was she running away?

At first, I thought it was because of her parents.

But this ... this was so much worse.

Bria became quiet, then finally turned toward me with tears in her eyes and wrapped her arms around my waist, pulling me close and letting her tears fall against my chest. "I'm sorry, Callum. I'm sorry that I brought this here. I shouldn't have ever come to this university. I shouldn't have agreed to office hours. I have done nothing but put you in danger."

I wrapped my arms around her and growled at my pack to disperse back through the forest. And even Adan and his pack gave us some privacy by following them. When they were all gone, I grasped Bria's face and forced her to look up at me.

"Can you please tell me what's going on?"

"I only know them by The Council, not The Wolf Council. But ... they're after me."

"Why?" I asked, brows furrowed.

"I don't know," she whispered, placing her hands over mine and biting back another sob. "But three months before I was supposed to go off to college, my parents sold me to them."

Chapter Thirty

BRIA

"So, what happened between you and Adan?" Jasmine asked, grabbing potato salad.

I took the spoon from her once she was finished and gnawed on the inside of my cheek. If she and Adan were mates, I really didn't think that she would want to know. I didn't want her to hate me, especially because we were close friends now.

"We dated," I finally said, knowing that I shouldn't lie to her. "Not for that long."

Jasmine pressed her lips together. "Did you really?"

"Yes," I said, turning toward her. "It was a long time ago."

To me, it felt like forever ago, but really, it was only mere weeks since the last time we were together. I had tried so hard to forget that night, but it was ingrained in my memory forever.

The blood on his hands. The smile on his face. The nerves zipping through my body.

The last time I saw Adan, he had ripped my brother's throat out of his neck and told me to run fast and far away from there and to never come back.

After a couple moments, we walked back to the quiet picnic table. We sat in the pack house's backyard, eating dinner with Adan's pack. Nobody spoke a single word to each other, the silence deafening and overwhelming. Callum pulled me closer to him at the picnic table as I tried to let his sweatshirt swallow me whole.

Less than twenty minutes, I had admitted that my parents sold me to The Council.

And I had barely been able to keep it together. No matter what questions he asked me, all I could think was the absolute worst. Like Adan said, The Council *would* find me, and when they did, they'd do anything to get me back.

"Did you guys read the last chapter?" a pup whispered a bit too loudly across the backyard, holding up the *One Alpha* from his backpack enough to show them the title on the cover. "It was—"

"Quiet down," a woman scolded them, nervously glancing at Adan. "And put that away."

"It's fine," Adan said, waving it off and giving her the most menacing smile—even though he probably thought it was a sweet one. "I don't give a fuck about The Council. All my pack members read that book too."

Adan glanced over at me like he did for the fiftieth time today, but I kept my gaze on the plate of untouched food in front of me, inching closer to Callum to show him that though Adan and I might've dated before, I didn't have any feelings for him now.

After getting the go-ahead from his mother, the boy pulled the book out of his backpack and lay on his stomach with a couple of other boys, talking about how the One Alpha was *so cool* and *so strong* and how they all wanted to be like him one day.

"Why did they do it?" Callum asked Adan, referring to my parents selling me to those assholes without explicitly stating it. He might've trusted his pack mates, but that didn't mean that I trusted them with this secret. "You have to know something."

Adan placed his hand on Jasmine's knee. "If I did, I would've taken care of it."

"They're going to find me here," I said, my stomach twisting in knots. I stared emptily at the food and felt bile rise in my throat. I clutched my empty stomach and pushed away the tears. "They're going to fucking find me and take me away."

I had been so stupid, thinking that I was safe here.

I put Callum and this entire pack in danger.

Callum wrapped his hand around the side of my face and forced me to look over at him. "Nobody is going to take you away from me," he said to me, gently leaning his forehead against mine. "I won't let anyone take you, no matter if it's The Council or not."

More tears welled up in my eyes. Mom and Dad had said that same thing, and then ... they sold me for a couple million dollars. When they saw that money, nothing else seemed to even matter anymore.

Not even me.

And I didn't want that to happen with Callum too.

I fucking loved him.

"We love him," that voice said in my head again.

Quickly, I tried to push the tears from my cheeks and to stop crying. All I wanted to do was run away from here. I didn't want these problems anymore. I didn't want to put Callum in danger. I wanted to disappear.

"Mate will protect us from everyone."

That voice was ... wrong—so wrong.

Adan swallowed hard and motioned for Jasmine to follow him elsewhere to give us privacy. At least, he wasn't being a dick to Callum anymore. In the past half hour, they had found some kind of peace between each other.

When they were gone, I curled my arms around Callum again and moved closer to him, not wanting to ever lose him. "You wanted to know more about my parents ..." I started. "They are nothing but assholes who abused me. They told me one thing and did another. They refused to let me be happy. They sold me for money. That's who they are, and that's who they will always be."

Callum held on to me tightly, his body tensing. "I'll kill them."

"They're untouchable and have The Council's protection. You can't."

"I will."

I pressed my lips together. "I'm afraid that you'll sell me out too. That you'll tell me lies."

Deep down, I knew that he would never do something like that. But I had been conditioned all my fucking life that I wasn't good enough, that I needed to be this or to be that, that I was the perfect daughter but the worst daughter at the same time.

It had been nonstop with my parents.

So bad to the point that, sometimes, I didn't even believe my own thoughts.

"I would never do that to you, Bria," he said, pulling away and looking down into my eyes. "You're my mate, and I would sacrifice my life before I allowed someone to take you away from me."

"Tell him that we would do the same. Tell him that we love him."

But I couldn't get the words out of my mouth. I wanted to assure him, too, but I was too terrified of The Council to believe myself anymore. If they wanted his head, they would take it, no matter how hard I tried to keep him safe.

And because Adan was here ... I was sure they were close behind.

Chapter Thirty-One

CALLUM

"Why are you getting up so early?" Bria asked, turning away from the window and pulling me down into the bed with her. "Come, sleep with me a bit more. We have all morning. Class doesn't start for"—she opened one eye and glanced at the digital clock—"like, two hours."

"I have a meeting this morning," I said. "Go to school with Levi and Jasmine."

"Please, stay," she whined, digging her *claws* into my forearm. "Pleeeease."

After kissing her head, I peeled her off me and walked to my closet to grab a shirt and tie. "If I start missing meetings and classes because you want me to stay with you, people are going to get suspicious. Not everyone in the school is a wolf, Bria. They don't understand *this*."

And by *this*, I meant this growing, intensifying connection between us.

Sure, if I taught in a werewolf-only school, things would be different. But there weren't many of them anymore. Mainly because

The Council didn't want anyone to learn all together and get ideas that they couldn't suppress. It was ridiculous.

I balled my hands into fists and continued to dress for the day.

When Adan and I could get more packs to agree to go to war with The Council, then I would gladly destroy them piece by piece. But until then, I had to prepare my pack and wait. Bria was right. If The Council came at us now, I wouldn't be able to destroy them.

No wolf, no alpha, no pack was strong enough to destroy them by themselves.

"Fine," Bria mumbled. "But you're going to get it later."

"Mmhmm, and how am I going to get it?" I asked, leaning against the doorframe and smiling at my mate's sleeping face.

She groggily opened her eyes and squinted at me, her eyes glowing enough for me to see the wolf inside of her, already ready to come out and see the world as her own being. "You'll see."

After giving her a laugh, I walked down the corridor to the back door, ran a hand through my hair, and sighed.

What was worse about this whole thing was that if The Council found out that she was a wolf now, they would have even more of a reason to try to take her from me and destroy her piece by piece.

Hell, nobody knew what they wanted with a human girl now.

"You'll never figure out why they want her," Adan said, slipping out of one of the spare rooms that I let his pack sleep in for the past couple days.

Part of me loathed the thought of him in the same house as his ex-girlfriend and my mate, but he was here to protect her.

At least, that was what I fucking hoped.

"It doesn't make sense," I said between clenched teeth, walking out of the pack house.

"It never has," Adan said, following me through the woods and down the path toward the university. "I've been trying to figure it out for months. I even killed her brother to get information out of him about why his parents would trade his sister. But none of them ever gave me anything."

"The Council hates humans mating with wolves. Why would a group of wolves want a human?" I asked myself, shaking my head and trying to wrap my mind around it. Yet the more I thought about it, the less and less it made any sense.

"I know you don't want to hear it because you're her mate, but ..." Adan paused and blew out a deep breath. "Their leader, Thiago Medina, has always had a thing for her. He had been the one to convince The Council to bring her in and pay her parents an absurd amount of money for her."

Shit.

Not that fucker.

When Thiago was younger, he had been the strongest advocate to ban the *One Alpha* and numerous other books that suppressed the werewolf species into thriving. He wanted complete control of the wolves and didn't want any of us to revolt against him.

I had met him once during a meeting with all the alphas in North America, and I hated him then. Now, I loathed that man more than anything. But one thing was fucking certain: I would not let him lay a hand on my Bria.

"If we find out what he wants with her, we'll know how to stop him," Adan said.

"How do you suppose we do that?" I snapped, spotting the school in the distance.

"I'll come up with something," he said.

I stopped in my tracks, turning toward him. "Why are you doing this?" I asked him. "Why are you still trying to protect Bria now that you have found your mate and she has found hers? You're no longer together anymore, and I don't like how comfortable you are with her."

Adan paused and growled, "Because Bria helped me out of a lot of shit that you don't need to know about. I'm not doing this out of the goodness of my heart. I don't try to lead like the One alpha, like you do. I hurt people, and I've wanted to hurt The Council for far too long."

"And Jasmine?" I asked. "You'd better not hurt her in the process. She's my wolf before she is your mate. It's my job to protect her too."

"Jasmine ..." Adan trailed off, staring back through the woods at the path we had walked. "She's my mate. And, like with Bria, I would do anything to protect her, too, which is why I'm not stopping until The Council is defeated. They're not just after Bria now that I killed her brother; they're going to be after me and Jasmine too."

For the first time, I almost felt bad for the alpha.

I recognized that look on his face. I understood that fear of not being able to protect the one woman that he loved the most. It was close to helplessness, pain, sorrow, and agony. The unknown was never too far behind.

"If you screw me over, I will kill you," I warned. "I won't hold back like I had last week."

"I don't expect you to," Adan said. "We're going to defeat these bastards and go our separate ways. Deal?"

He held out a hand for me to shake.

I grabbed it and squeezed. "Deal."

Chapter Thirty-Two

BRIA

After Callum left for his meeting, I dressed in a short plaid skirt and a sweatshirt with the university's name across the chest. Then, I begged Jasmine and Levi to walk to school early with me because I was a bit annoyed at Callum and maybe a bit hornier than usual.

We sat in the classics library, waiting for mythology class. And I might have possibly snuck out of the library when they weren't looking and tiptoed down the hallways to Professor Lee's office. I leaned my ear against the door and knocked, really hoping his meeting hadn't started yet.

"Come in," Callum called.

When I peeked my head into the door, Callum raised his brows. "I thought I told you to stay with Jasmine and Levi."

"They're in the library." I stepped into the room and closed the door behind me. "But I snuck away from them to come see you."

"How many times do I have to tell you that you need to stay with them?" he asked.

"Many," I admitted, walking around his desk toward him. "But … I'm horny."

I leaned against his desk, slid my ass onto it, and maneuvered my way in front of him, so each of my legs were on either side of his, my short plaid skirt doing nothing to hide my glistening cunt. After spreading my legs a bit wider, I smiled at him.

"I'm not wearing any underwear today," I murmured to him. "And I know how much you're dying to eat my cunt, *Professor Lee*. I wanted to tease you during class and pull up my skirt enough for you to see, but … I need you now."

"Bria, I have a meeting with Chancellor Wilmar in five minutes," Callum said.

"But, *Professor*, don't your needy students come first?" I teased, leaning back on one hand and drawing two fingers up my wet pussy. Then, I stuck my fingers into his mouth and whimpered. "I need help with the material."

"Bria," Callum said, voice teetering on the edge of total loss of control.

I grasped his tie and pulled him closer to me. "Professor."

Heat gathered in my core, and I let a whimper escape through my lips, knowing that it would bring out his ferocious, hungry wolf. And when it did, I slipped two fingers between my pussy lips again and spread them apart.

"I see that hungry look in your eyes. You want to eat my cunt so badly, don't you?"

"If you don't leave now, you're not going to like the consequences when we get home."

"Oh …" I rubbed my aching clit for him. "I'm so scared."

"Bria."

"Isn't your job to help your students out?" I asked, grasping his chin with my wet fingers and forcing him to finally look at my sopping pussy. "Help me out, Professor. Eat my pussy, so I can focus in your class today."

"You're going to get me in so much trouble," he said before he wrapped his arms around my thighs and pulled me to the edge of the desk, resting my thighs on his shoulders and burying his face between my legs.

I fell back on his desk, my legs trembling already. All morning, I had been aching for him to touch me like this.

He flicked his tongue out against my clit, my juices decorating his thick scruff. I leaned my head back and laced a hand in his hair, moving my hips back and forth against his mouth to get off. He pinned my hips to the desk and moved his tongue even faster against me, making me moan aloud.

I slapped a hand to my mouth to suppress my moans and clenched. "Please, fuck me, Professor," I begged. "Bend me over your desk and punish me with your cock for disobeying you. Teach me to never do this again."

"Bria," he growled, thrusting his fingers into me, "we have two minutes."

"What? You don't think you can punish the teacher's pet in two minutes?" I asked, wanting him to get angry. "You must not be a good enough—"

Before I could finish my sentence, he pulled me off the desk, flipped me over onto my stomach, and pulled down his zipper. Smacking me hard on the ass, he thrust his huge cock into my tight and aching hole. After wrapping his other hand around the front of my throat, he pulled me off the desk and strummed his fingers.

"When we get home, you're going to fucking get it, Bria," he growled into my ear.

"What is the big, bad alpha going to do to me?" I asked breathlessly, tightening even more on him. "Tie me up and have his way with me?" Just the thought made me so close to exploding all over him. "Mark my neck again and claim me? Put his mouth over every inch of my body?"

Callum tightened his hand around my throat and smacked my tit through my sweatshirt, his canines grazing against my neck. "Your filthy little mouth doesn't know when to stop. You want me to punish you harder than I have before, don't you, Bria?"

The pressure rose in my core. "Yes."

Someone knocked on the door. "Professor Lee, is now a good time?"

"Fuck," Callum cursed against me. "One moment! I'm with a student."

"More like pounding your first-year's pussy raw," I said.

"I'm going to come in your cunt, Bria," Callum growled into my ear. "And you're going to hold it there all class. And if any—*any*—slides down your thighs while you're walking, taking notes, giving a presentation today, you're going to let it."

My pussy tightened even more around him.

"Do you understand me?" he whispered into my ear.

"Yes," I whimpered.

After a couple more thrusts, Callum slammed into me and stilled. He slapped a hand over my mouth, and I moaned into it, my core exploding with pleasure. Wave after wave of ecstasy shot through me. When he pulled out of me, I inhaled sharply and pressed my sticky legs together.

He gave me such a huge load that I could already feel it dripping down my thighs from under my skirt. I smoothed out my clothes and walked to his office door, opening it up and smiling at the chancellor in the hallway, typing away on his phone.

"Good morning, Chancellor Wilmar." I gave him a smile, hoping that I didn't look like I just fucked my professor, and walked past him toward my first class. "Have a great day! I know I will."

Chapter Thirty-Three

CALLUM

When I told Bria to let my cum run down her thighs, I didn't think she'd actually listen. But when she walked down the walkway of my classroom toward the front row with Jasmine and Levi, her thighs were still covered with my cum.

And her little pussy was still salivating for my cock. As soon as she sat in the front row, the scent hit me harder than Adan had the other day in the forest. I grasped the edges of the standing desk and cursed to myself.

"How was your morning, Professor Lee?" Bria teased, giving me a small smile in front of all these other human students. She wanted to break me yet again today, and if she kept this up, she would.

Don't get me wrong; I loved teaching mythology, but my mate's scent was so much better than anything I had ever smelled before. So much so that it drove me over the edge nearly every single time. Which meant one thing: Bria's wolf was growing quickly.

After I had marked her, everything became way more intense.

And now, this feeling was only growing.

Most human turned werewolves didn't shift until their first full moon, which would've meant that we had nearly a month before Bria shifted, but she had been getting stronger so much faster than any other human I had seen. It was unreal.

So far, I had seen glimpses of her wolf, and I couldn't wait until I met her.

"It was good, Miss Benton," I said, shuffling through some papers and feeling my eyes shift slightly.

My wolf wanted out, wanted to devour every inch of her body right here and right now. I didn't want to wait any longer.

"Is it okay if I sit here?" someone said to Jasmine, pulling me out of my little trance.

Levi, Jasmine, and Bria glanced over at a boy with thick black glasses, pimples, and about ten mythology books in his hands.

"I just transferred and wanted to make sure nobody else was sitting here."

Jasmine smiled at him and moved her backpack in front of her legs to give him room. "Sure! Not many people like sitting in the front, so all these seats are pretty much empty. What's your name? Isn't it a bit late to change classes?"

I eyed him and pressed my lips together. Jasmine was right. It was too late to switch classes; the two-week period was over, which meant that nobody new should be transferring into my class unless they had gotten clearance from Chancellor Wilmar. And the chancellor didn't mention anything this morning about a new student.

But that asshole loved giving me trouble either way.

Levi rolled his eyes. "Didn't *you* just switch into this class?"

"Why don't you shut your mouth, Levi?" Jasmine snarled. "I'm trying to be friendly."

The boy laughed awkwardly and scratched the back of his head, glancing at Bria. "I kinda sucked up to Chancellor Wilmar to switch out of calculus. I'm not the best at math, which I've quickly found out. Anyway, I'm Holden."

"Hi, Holden." Bria stuck out her hand for him to shake. "I'm Bria."

When he took her hand, I nearly let a growl slip through my lips. I balled my hands into fists behind the standing desk and cleared my throat.

"Sit down," I said a bit too harshly to the class. "Class is beginning."

Yet, all class, I kept an eye on Holden. I didn't know what it was, but something was off about him. Maybe I was too fucking possessive of Bria, but still, that didn't seem like the only explanation. Holden might've seemed into her, but there was something more, something else.

"Holden," I called after class, before he could pack his belongings. "Can I talk to you?"

Holden looked over his shoulder, scurried over to me with his hands stuffed into his pockets, and smiled. "Hi, Professor Lee. I'm Holden. I transferred into this class last minute with Chancellor Wilmar's approval. I hope you don't mind."

"What class are you coming from?"

"Calculus."

"Which professor?"

"Uh, he had a long gray beard, bushy eyebrows."

"Professor Garett?" I asked Holden.

Professor Garett was a female English professor that had never even set foot in the mathematics building.

"Yeah, that's him," Holden said, pushing up his glasses again. "I couldn't focus in there."

I pressed my lips together, still unable to figure him out. Why was he lying? More importantly, why had he transferred into this class? He was a human who had no excuse to really be here. And he surely wasn't part of Adan's pack at all.

"You shouldn't have transferred. You'll need to make up an exam," I said.

"No problem," Holden said, walking back over to his desk and clapping his hands on the stack of mythology textbooks he had taken from the library. "I've been studying for this class all weekend and catching up on all the work on the syllabus. I'll be ready to take it at the end of this week."

"Great," I said between clenched teeth.

Fucking great.

"We're going to have lunch on the quad," Jasmine said to him. "You're welcome to join."

He hiked his backpack onto his shoulders and pushed up his glasses, nervously scratching his neck under his sweater, pulling it down enough to display the tattoo he had on his shoulder. And it wasn't any tattoo.

It was a symbol of The Council.

Chapter Thirty-Four

BRIA

"Bria," Callum shouted from his standing desk in front of the class.

I stopped and glanced over my shoulder. Jasmine, Levi, and Holden paused, too, all turning around to stare at our professor, who looked more tense than he had after I told him that I dated Adan.

"Can I speak with you for a moment?"

"Sure," I said, staring uneasily between Jasmine and Levi. Then, I glanced at Holden, who looked right at Callum, like he knew something was up between us. "Why don't you guys get lunch without me? I'll catch up later. It was nice meeting you, Holden."

Holden snapped his head back to me and plastered a fake smile on his face. "You too, Bria. Maybe we could get lunch some other time together, and you can catch me up on what I've missed so far."

"Uh, maybe."

Jasmine curtly nodded to Callum, then turned back to Levi and Holden, gesturing to the exit doors of the classroom. "Come on. We know this really good place that sells hot wings. If you're a fan, you'll love them, Holden."

When they disappeared through the doors, after Holden glanced back at Callum and me, I cut my gaze to Callum and opened my mouth to ask him what was going on. Holden didn't give me the creeps, but he did make me a bit uneasy.

Before I could get out a word, Callum slapped a hand over my mouth and nodded to a side door, gesturing for me not to say anything until we reached his office. I pressed my lips together and followed him out the door, scanning our surroundings to see if anyone was watching.

After we stepped into his office, Callum locked the door and blew out a deep breath. He drew his tongue across his now-extended canines and let out a low, guttural growl, his claws cutting right into his palms.

"Stay away from that guy," Callum said to me. "He's part of The Council."

My chest tightened, my entire body frozen.

No. They couldn't have found me already. I couldn't go back. I refused to go back.

I stared at Callum through watery eyes and bit back a sob, my entire world collapsing in on me. He stood tensely, his chest moving up and down unsteadily and his teeth glistening with saliva, like a wild animal.

Callum might've been my professor. He might've been a ruthless alpha werewolf.

But I ... I had fallen in love with him. I couldn't lose him.

Unable to stop myself, I wrapped my arms around his taut waist and pulled him closer to me, resting my head on his chest and sobbing into his dress shirt. Every emotion that I had buried from the past few years suddenly hit me at once.

Terror. Anxiety. Rage. Misery.

Fuck. I balled his shirt into my fists. *I refuse to lose him.*

I would not be the weak girl that The Council remembered me

as. I would train to get strong for as long as I had left. I would fight them until my very last breath. With this new guy in my class, my days were limited.

But I would work my fucking ass off.

Nobody would hurt my friends and family again because of me.

"I'm going to take care of you," Callum said, gently grasping my face and tilting my head to look up at him. The sunlight flooded into his room, illuminating every thick hair on his jaw and making his hazel eyes a hundred shades of magical gold. "You don't have to worry."

And while I'd still worry, warmth spread throughout my chest.

Never in my life had anyone told me they would take care of me and meant it.

Hearing those words from him both scared me and actually made me feel ... good for the first time ever. Callum wasn't going to run away or turn me in or hurt me in any way. He was going to stick by my side and fight.

My mate.

"Our mate." A small voice broke through the doubts and worries.

I stared up at Callum and dragged my fingers through his thick and dark scruff, a low hum rumbling from deep within my chest, one that I wasn't controlling.

"There is a voice inside my head," I whispered, hoping he didn't think I was crazy.

Callum's stoic look suddenly softened, and a smile graced his face. "Your wolf."

I swallowed hard, my stomach fluttering with excitement. "I think so."

He pushed some hair off my forehead with his index finger. "What does she say to you?"

My lips curled into a smile, my cheeks flushing. Giddiness rushed through my body, and something stirred inside me—a beast waiting to finally come to life. Goddess, I felt like I had when Professor Lee emailed me the first time with that book suggestion.

Somehow, even then, Callum made me feel so special.

"Hmm?" Callum asked, seizing the small of my hips, picking me up into the air with total ease, and setting me on his desk. He placed one large hand beside my thigh and buried his face into the crook of my neck, his scruff tickling my skin. "What's she saying to you about me?"

"That you're definitely not her type," I teased him.

He growled into my ear, making me both giggle and clench at the sound of a possessive alpha—*my* possessive alpha. He slid his hands up the sides of my thighs and maneuvered his way between my legs, tugging me closer to the edge.

"Well, she'd better get used to me because I'm not leaving her."

I rested my forehead against his and smiled. "You promise?"

"I promise you, Bria," he said to me, his voice softening. "I'm never going to leave you."

Chapter Thirty-Five

CALLUM

"He didn't say anything," Jasmine said, sitting down in my office and letting out a sigh.

"Nothing?" I asked, brows creased together.

Surely, Holden had something to say about my Bria. If he really was with The Council, he would've at least tried to make a move today at lunch, asked about her schedule, or who she roomed with here. He needed to get information—at least, that was what I thought.

"All he asked was if Bria had a boyfriend."

I balled my hands into fists. I'd kill that fucking boy now.

Levi strolled in with his hands stuffed into his jeans pockets. "Maybe he asked *you* that, Jasmine, but we had a pretty lengthy conversation while you were in the bathroom, freaking out that we were talking to someone from The Council."

Jasmine rolled her eyes. "Ugh, *you* holding an intelligent conversation. Since when?"

"Actually, I have intelligent conversations all the time. I just dumb myself down for you."

After punishing Levi hard in the arm, Jasmine growled and turned back to me with her lips pressed together in a tight line. "I couldn't get any information out of him either. He was so tight-lipped about everything, even his past. He was almost too convincing."

"And if Bria didn't recognize him, maybe he recently joined The Council," Levi said, sitting beside Jasmine and shrugging his shoulders. "When I talked to him, he only asked about Bria a couple of times. Nothing that you would particularly want to hear about."

"Like what?" I asked, raising my brow.

"Nothing," Levi said.

"Levi," I growled. "*What*?"

He grimaced. "You know, like ... how attractive Bria is. He wanted to know if I ever had a thing with her. Stuff like that. He said that he thought she was pretty and some other weird shit along those lines. Stuff you won't want to hear as her mate."

My canines ripped through my gums, and I growled again, hungry for blood.

Who did this fucker think he was? Bria would never go for someone like him.

She was mine.

"What'd you say?"

Levi cringed again and hiked his thumb back to the door. "I think I'm going to—"

"If you even move to stand up without spilling, I will give you more pack duties than you already have. Don't fucking make me angry, Levi. You know not to piss me off, but you keep doing it anyway."

Once he let out a long-drawn-out sigh, Levi stared at my desk and refused to look me in the eye. "You can't get mad at me because *you said* that we should try to get along well with him to get information. So, that's what I did."

Jasmine smacked him on the back of the head. "He doesn't want your explanation."

Levi winced. "Fine. Fine. I, um"—he scratched his neck—"might've agreed with him."

Before I could stop myself, I was halfway across the room with Levi's neck in my hands.

"You did what?" I growled between tight lips, pissed off that the one damn guy I asked to help me out decided to by telling the enemy that my mate was hot.

I knew how guys talked to one another about she-wolves.

I had been that young before. I had done it, too, at one point.

Not anymore.

And I especially didn't want anyone talking about my mate like that.

"I didn't know what else to say to him. I was trying to get on his good side, so he'd, you know, spill what he was going to do with Bria. I didn't mean anything that I said about Bria being sexy—I mean, she is, but I—"

Jasmine snatched Levi's ear between her fingers and dragged him out of my hold to my office door. "You don't know when to keep your big mouth shut. All you do is make things worse. I wouldn't be surprised if Holden now knows we're onto him."

"He doesn't," I said.

If he did, the entire Council would be here now.

"Who doesn't what?" Adan said, opening my office door and strolling into the room.

When he slid his arm around Jasmine's waist, she let go of Levi's ear and immediately fell into him, her lips curling into a small smile.

As much as I hated that fucking man, I could only wish that I had met Bria when I was his age. He would get to spend the rest of his life with Jasmine, sixty to seventy years with her. And while I would spend the rest of my life with Bria, I didn't have that kind of time. I was so much older than she was.

"We have a problem," I said to him, walking to my seat behind my desk again. "Someone who's a part of The Council showed up in my classroom today, sat right in the front row beside these guys, and asked about Bria."

"Fuck," Adan said, running a hand through his hair. "They're fucking here already?"

"We don't think he knows much yet or even has a plan. Levi and I went out to lunch—"

Adan snapped his head toward me, canines lengthened. "You fucking let my mate go out to lunch with someone in The fucking Council?! Are you fucking kidding me, Lee? You don't even know how fucking dangerous that is."

Jasmine scrunched up her face. "I'm a big girl."

"No, you're not," Adan said. "Not big enough to face them alone. Not even one of them."

"There wasn't a way to get them all out of it without seeming suspicious," I said, digging my claws into my palms.

If I had called them all back to talk, Holden would have known that something fishy was up. And I wanted him to stumble a bit, so I could catch him and hold something over The Council's heads.

"It was dangerous," I admitted. "But we needed something."

"That doesn't mean you fucking put my mate in danger."

I slammed my hands on the desk. "Well, they don't want your mate! They want mine."

"And Bria is my friend," Jasmine said. "I won't let them take her. I'll do whatever it takes."

"Me too," Levi chirped in.

Adan glared at me, then at Jasmine, then over his shoulder. "Where's Bria now?"

"In the library," I said.

He shut the door with his foot and turned back to us. "Then, we need to make a plan. One that doesn't involve her. She's scared but stubborn and will do anything to protect the people she loves."

Chapter Thirty-Six

BRIA

"You know what I don't understand, Alpha?" I said, rolling onto my stomach in Callum's bed with nothing but his T-shirt covering my body. I drew my finger across the sheets and smiled at him standing in the doorway with dark circles under his eyes that somehow made him look sexier. "Why you're not between my legs."

Callum stared at me with those hazel eyes, pulled on his collar to loosen it, and chuckled, shutting the door behind him as he walked into the room closer and closer to me. The moonlight flooded into the room, glinting against his face so perfectly.

"One alpha," my wolf whispered through my mind, the sound so soft and so quiet that I almost didn't hear it.

I sucked in a sharp breath, running through the information I read in the stack of mythology books I found in Callum's library.

Sculpted jaw, strong nose, and even those dangerous eyes.

If anyone resembled the man from the book, it was my Callum.

After tugging off his tie, he undid his shirt button by button, his fingers moving swiftly down the center of his abdomen until the clothing hung loosely off his broad shoulders. I crawled up to the headboard and pressed my thighs together, watching *my mate.*

He unbuckled his belt, then unbuttoned his suit pants, the bulge in his pants nearly ripping open the zipper. I gulped at the sight of him, remembering how my professor felt inside of me earlier today.

But one time wasn't enough.

Merely a couple of weeks ago, I hadn't even spent the night like this with anyone. Now, I needed Callum's dick twice a day. Soon enough, I'd be needing it every single moment of every single day, just because.

He stalked closer and crawled onto the bed toward me, wrapping his arms around my thighs and pulling me to him until I lay flat against the mattress. He rested on his stomach, drawing his nose up my inner thigh to my core.

"Wait until you go into heat," Callum said, as if he read my mind.

"Heat?" I whispered, eyes wide. "What's that?"

Warm breath on my pussy, he gently brushed his lips over my clit. I sucked in a sharp breath, heat spreading through my core like a damn wildfire, burning me up from the inside out, a sensation that only grew even more when he was close to me.

"Do you feel that heat between your legs when I touch you here?" Callum asked, dipping his head and gently kissing my clit, sending another wave of warmth throughout my body.

I whimpered and tried to press my thighs together, my clit sensitive tonight. "Yes."

"When you go through heat"—he kissed my inner thigh—"your little pussy heats your entire body"—another kiss, closer to my aching cunt—"and you become a wild, feral she-wolf, hungry for my cum."

He kissed me again, this time on the pussy lips, and I ached for him to draw his tongue over my clit again. I laced a hand through his thick dark brown hair and pulled him closer to my pussy, moving my hips up and down gently.

"You won't be able to stop yourself from crawling on top of me and riding me until your body can't handle any more." He pushed a finger inside me and stared up at me with those sinful eyes, the way he always did when he was about to say something filthy. "And even then, you won't stop, Bria. You'll be too desperate to have my pups in your stomach."

My eyes widened, and I sucked in another breath. "Pups?"

"Babies."

"Babies," I whispered.

"Your pussy just got so tight and wet for me." Callum slowly pushed another finger into me. "Do you like the thought of me filling you with so much cum one night until your belly becomes swollen?"

He thrust in and out of me, teasing my G-spot with his long, rough fingers.

I squirmed on him, the pressure almost too much to handle already, and grasped the bedsheets in my fists. "Please."

"Answer me, Bria," he said.

I stared down into his lovely, hungry hazel eyes, wanting nothing more than for him to shove his face between my legs and eat my pussy until I covered his mouth in my juices for the second time today.

"You want me to eat your pussy again," Callum said, reading my mind once more.

"Yes."

His fingers stilled inside me. "Then, answer me."

They lay upon my G-spot, and I knew that one little, fine movement would send me over the edge, screaming with pleasure, in my classics professor's bed.

"Callum ..."

"Bria," he purred, "be a good girl and answer."

"Yes," I nearly shouted. "Yes!"

The mere sound of the words made me gasp for breath. I barely knew Callum for a month, and I already wanted to carry his pups?! I barely knew the damn guy. This damn wolf was really—

"Oh my God!" I moaned loudly, the pleasure rushing through me.

Callum curled his fingers over and over against my G-spot, even after the first initial shock of ecstasy, and sucked my clit into his mouth, drawing his tongue back and forth over the sensitive bud.

Suddenly, Callum turned us over, so he lay back on the bed, and I sat on his face. While the pleasure rushed through me, I gasped, still self-conscious and hating the thought of being on top of him. I weighed more than any of these she-wolves in his pack, not by that much, but probably by a good thirty to forty pounds at least.

And, damn, I didn't want him to see me from this angle.

But Callum seemed not to care, as he continued to eat my cunt like he had been waiting decades to taste his mate. He moved his hands up my body, grasping and tugging and kneading anyplace that he could get his hands on, my love handles and all.

"Callum," I murmured, my legs trembling around his shoulders, "I'm going to come."

Again.

"Without my cum inside you?" he asked, tugging on both my nipples.

I grasped the headboard and dug my claws right through the wood, screaming out to the moon from how intense the pressure was flooding through my body. I arched my back, the pleasure suddenly replaced by an intense pain all over.

My vision suddenly shifted, becoming more intense in the darkness of the night. My canines lengthened in my mouth, blood pouring from my gums at the harsh transformation. Callum noticed the tenseness of my body and moved beside me, his brows furrowed together.

Unable to stop myself, I grasped his throat and drew my canines up the side of his neck. "Mine," I growled. "All mine."

Chapter Thirty-Seven

CALLUM

Bria wrapped her hand around my throat and thrust me against the headboard, her claws sinking into my skin and her canines grazing against my neck. I inhaled sharply at the feel of her wolf finally coming out to play with mine.

"Mine," she growled, sniffing my neck and holding on to me even tighter. "All mine."

My body shivered, and I tucked a strand of hair behind her ear. "Bria ..."

When she moved back enough to look me in the eye, gold pooled in her eyes, the color spinning and whirling around her pupils, mixing with her blue-violet irises and slowly—very slowly—overtaking them.

It wasn't like anything I had ever seen before. Irises didn't move like that.

"Mine," Bria said, a low grumble rumbling through her chest. "You're mine."

I placed my hand over hers, which was around my neck, to loosen her grip on me. While I knew that she didn't mean to hurt me and that this was her wolf taking control of her, she continued to squeeze harder by the second.

Just like she had during my fight with Adan.

"Bria, please, let up a bit," I said.

"Mine," she growled louder this time, squeezing even tighter.

"Mate wants to mark us," my wolf whispered through my mind, aching me to surrender control to him, so they could be together finally.

He had waited as long as I had, and while I remained in control for the past forty-three years, he could barely contain his excitement around her.

"Reassure her that we're hers. Give me control."

With my hand around hers, I tilted my head to the side. For the past forty-three long years, I had been imagining what it'd feel like when my mate marked me back. I had heard stories of the overwhelming feeling shooting through the body.

But had yet to experience it.

Though I so desperately wanted to feel her canines sink into my neck, our bond to finally be complete. I didn't want to wait anymore, and neither did my wolf. What happened tonight was something that I would remember forever.

"I'm yours," I whispered.

Bria let up slightly, her growls turning into cute little purrs.

"I'm all yours, Bria," I murmured. "Mark me."

Bria ran her teeth up and down the column of my neck again, stopping where my neck met my shoulder and inhaling deeply. My eyes fluttered back, and I tightened my hand around hers, desperately aching for it.

"Please. Mark me. Do it. I want to feel you."

Alphas never begged for anything.

But, fuck, I was pleading for it.

Crawling onto me, Bria straddled my waist and drew her tongue across my skin. Shivers ran through me, goose bumps rising on my skin. I grunted into her ear, my dick still rock fucking hard against her quivering pussy.

"Mark you," she mumbled against my skin, the tops of her teeth pricking me.

"Claim me."

"Claim you ..."

Suddenly, Bria froze and gasped. She pulled her hands away from my throat at lightning speed and scrambled back to the other side of the bed, staring at my neck with wide blue-violet eyes again. Those swimming gold irises had completely disappeared.

Her wolf was gone.

Without marking me.

"Callum, I'm ..." she started breathlessly. "I'm so sorry. I didn't mean to hurt you."

When she glanced down at her hands, she screamed. Blood covered her fingers and rolled down to her palms. I reached up to feel the tiny little claw marks in my neck that must've been bleeding at one point but were now completely healed.

"I ..." Tears welled up in her eyes. "You're bleeding because of me."

"It's okay, Bria," I said, keeping my voice low so she wouldn't get startled.

I went to move toward her, but she scrambled even further back to the edge of the bed. She stared at my mark for a couple moments, shaking her head in fear, then placed her hand into mine.

"I'm sorry," she said again.

Pulling her closer to me, I set her in my lap and showed her my neck. "It's healed. Don't be sorry. Your wolf lost control for a bit—that's all. You don't have to worry about hurting me. You're my mate. Your wolf won't allow you to."

"B-but—"

Knowing that the thought of growing claws and canine teeth for the first time must've been fucking terrifying, I pulled her closer to me and laid her on my chest, gently moving my fingers through her hair and letting her cry.

As I stared out the window and up at the moon, I smiled and silently thanked the Moon Goddess for granting me Bria Benton. Out of all the people she could've paired me up with, the Goddess we worshipped paired me with this beautiful, strong woman.

And soon, her first shift would be upon us.

Usually, new wolves didn't shift or show *this* much aggression until the first full moon after their bite. But Bria—I stared at her in amazement and cracked an even bigger smile—was far from a normal wolf. She was stronger than anyone else in my pack, maybe even me.

No wonder why Thiago, the leader of The Council, wanted her.

She could threaten his entire rule over that brainwashed group of idiots.

She could lead.

Chapter Thirty-Eight

BRIA

The next morning, I sat in the school library with my face stuffed into the mythology textbook for Callum's class. Since last night, after I nearly choked Callum to death, I wanted to forget. I didn't want my wolf to come back out for a long time because I didn't have control over her. So, I read every single page of the two-hundred-page textbook twice this morning already.

Anything to keep my mind occupied.

I didn't know why I kept losing control. By the look on Callum's face and what I heard from Jasmine, it wasn't natural to show this many signs of shifting before the first full moon. And as much as I wanted to control it, I didn't even know *when* it happened.

My human half seemed to black out completely.

"Hi, Bria," Holden said, taking a seat on the other side of the table.

Fuck.

What was he even doing here? Jasmine had left to go to class, and Levi wasn't even supposed to be here until four p.m., so we could walk back to Callum's pack house. I didn't want to be left alone with this asshole.

Swallowing hard, I stared at him with wide eyes and forced a smile on my face. "Hey."

"So, what'd Professor Lee want yesterday?" Holden asked, pulling out his laptop.

I anxiously rubbed my hands together under the table. "Nothing."

It was obvious that Callum wanted something, especially because I didn't meet them for lunch after he held me back at the end of class. And I didn't doubt that terror was written all over my face now because I sat across from a man who had access to The Council. If he didn't know that I knew about him, then, fuck, he would know now.

"Jasmine told me that you don't have a boyfriend," Holden said, glancing up from his computer screen.

"Nope."

"We have mate." My wolf spoke up for the first time since last night, and I tensed.

God, she couldn't be back already, could she? I didn't need her transforming right here in front of Holden and all these other human students.

"Tell him that we have a mate."

"No boyfriend," I repeated.

"What's a girl like you doing without a boyfriend in a school like this? You see how many couples are crawling all over campus." He chuckled and ran his hand through his thick hair. "It kinda freaks me out."

"Yeah, it freaks me out too."

Actually, *he* freaked me out more.

"Thank God I'm not the only one," he said, pulling a textbook out of his backpack—and not just any textbook, but the *One Alpha* book that Callum and Adan both stated was banned for the werewolf species.

Holden wasn't a werewolf—at least, I didn't think he was.

But why the hell did he have that, especially if The Council banned it?

"What's that?" I asked, playing stupid. "Is it for a class here?"

"Yeah," Holden said, eyes glinting gold.

I inhaled sharply at the sudden change of color in his eyes that I only ever saw in wolves. My stomach twisted and knotted, and I suddenly had the urge to puke up my lunch. Something felt terribly wrong.

God, I wished Jasmine had skipped class today.

"What class?" I asked, looking at my computer and acting like this was small talk.

He stared at me intently. "Mythology of Wolves."

This man was fucking with me.

Repeating to myself that I wouldn't slip up, I pressed my lips together. I didn't know what kind of game he was playing with me or what he was doing here from The Council. Was he patiently waiting for me to make a mistake? To blindly trust him?

Fuck no.

They must've thought I was stupid.

"Mythology of Wolves?" I asked, raising my brows and looking up at him. "Never heard of that class. It sounds kinda boring. Who teaches that?"

"Freddrick," Holden said without a pause, lying straight through his teeth.

Oh, he was good.

"Hanny Freddrick?" I asked.

"Yep. That's him. Pretty cool guy."

"He doesn't teach mythology," I said, continuing to type, as if it were nothing, like his lie didn't bother me. All I wanted was for him to fucking choke on his own words. "He teaches engineering."

"He's a new professor," Holden said, shoving the book back into his backpack.

There goes his studying for his mythology class. This guy was a joke.

"Cool," I said, not looking over at him and continuing my third go at the mythology textbook for Callum's class.

No matter how hard this guy tried, he wouldn't fucking break me. I refused to go back to The Council and see Thiago's ugly face.

That man thought he was a god or something.

I balled my hands into fists under the table and stared angrily at the words on the page, not really reading them, but focusing all my energy on coming up with a plan on how to get the fuck out of here. Holden obviously knew that I was onto him. He would become more aggressive soon.

And I didn't want to be anywhere near him when he did.

I refused to risk putting myself in danger of being alone with him somewhere *not* in public. But I had to get out of here *without* him following me. I had to contact someone, but Levi sucked at texting back, Jasmine didn't check her phone during class, and Callum was teaching.

I was all alone.

With this idiot.

For the next damn hour.

Chapter Thirty-Nine

CALLUM

Usually, Bria visited me during the day at around four p.m., before she and Levi left to go back to the pack house. But today, she didn't show up, and I was getting worried about where she could've gone off to.

Maybe nowhere. Maybe someone *took* her.

A growl rumbled from my chest, my canines lengthening. If anyone took my Bria, I would rip them to fucking shreds in front of whoever was around. I didn't care if the humans saw. Nobody touched her, except me.

Tearing off my shirt and changing into sweatpants, I stormed out of my office and ran toward the quad, where Bria used to sit when it was a bit warmer. Now that the fall breeze was rolling in, I doubted that she'd be there.

I ran around the quad twice and didn't spot Bria once. Instead, Jasmine stood with one of her friends, coming out of class with her books in her hand. Though I didn't want to make it suspicious, I walked up to her anyway.

"Have you seen Bria?" I asked.

She excused herself, walked with me a few feet away, and widened her eyes. "No, I haven't. What's going on?"

"Fuck," I growled, running a hand through my hair and inhaling deeply to see if Bria's scent lingered anywhere nearby. "I haven't talked to her since this morning. She comes to visit me before my last class every single day at four p.m. on the dot. Where the fuck is she?"

"Calm down, Alpha, before anyone—"

"Don't tell me to calm down," I snapped at her, rage rushing through every one of my veins. "She's my mate, and there is a fucking group of fiends who wants to kill her for some fucking reason. I need to find her."

If I fucking lost that woman, I would lose myself too.

"Maybe she's in the library," Jasmine said, glancing in the direction of the library on the other side of the quad. "She told me that she was going to keep busy today after what happened between you and her last night. She said that she ... kinda went crazy on you. She's scared it's going to happen again."

Fuck. That was another thing.

I thought I would have more time to prepare and teach her how to control herself.

With Bria being stronger than other wolves, she might start losing control here. Her body might try to make her shift in front of humans, and I didn't even think she knew that she was shifting into her wolf last night.

By the way she acted, her human side must've blacked out almost completely.

Almost as if on cue, Bria walked out of the library very tensely with Holden fucking next to her. I stormed over to them, wanting to get her out of that conversation as quickly as humanly possible. I didn't want her near that boy.

"Hey, Professor Lee," Holden said when I approached. "Bria and I were just studying for mythology class."

"Yeah, Holden is taking this really cool course," Bria said, giving me a get-me-out-of-here stare. "It's called the Mythology of Wolves with this weird textbook that has a wolf on it. It kinda reminded me of that myth we learned about in your class."

"Yeah, the textbook is called *One Alpha*," Holden said, smirking at me.

From the look in his eyes, I fucking knew that he knew we knew about him.

Something must've happened in the past few hours because he didn't look like he had a clue this morning during class. Maybe Bria slipped or ... she shifted into her wolf even if it was only a change in eye color.

Her ever-changing gold irises weren't something one could look at and ignore.

They screamed wolf.

Powerful wolf.

"Well, anyway, I'm off," Holden said, turning his back to me and glancing at Bria. "If you ever reconsider the whole boyfriend thing, I have a friend that I could introduce you to. He's seen a couple of pictures of you, and let's just say that he's *very* interested."

I bit my tongue and held back a vicious growl that clawed its way up my throat.

To my surprise, instead of shrinking back in fear, Bria hugged her books to her chest and stood tall. "Really? That's weird. I don't have any social media anymore. Where'd he see the pictures, Holden?"

Holden shrugged and stared at her, a golden glint in his eyes. "You know, *around*."

"What's your friend's name?" Bria asked.

"Thiago."

My heart dropped, a chill running through my bones. Thiago, leader of The Council.

"Well, why don't you tell *Thiago* that Bria Benton isn't interested in a man who has other people do his dirty work?" Bria said, pushing her shoulders back and staring him right in the eye. "Because I'm not interested in him or afraid of him. If he wants me, tell him to come get me himself."

Chapter Forty

BRIA

After Holden rudely told me—in front of Callum—that if I ever wanted a boyfriend, he'd contact Thiago, I stomped back to Callum's office with him, seething. Holden had some damn nerve to say that to me after everything that happened between The Council and me *and* while Callum was listening.

I didn't care anymore what The Council knew about me.

Flying into Callum's office, I paced around the room. It was obvious during my *nice chat* with Holden for the past few hours in the library that he knew that I knew about The Council and about him. He wasn't stupid, and neither was The Council. They were some of the smartest damn people that I'd ever met.

Holden probably knew that we figured it out the first day of class.

Maybe that was what he wanted.

Callum shut the door behind us and cleared his throat. "Bria, what was that?"

Eyes snapping open wide, I turned on my heel toward him. "What was what?"

"You talked so bluntly to Holden about The Council. You're putting yourself in danger."

For the first time ever, I snapped at Callum. I couldn't hold myself back. I had so much anger built up inside me from seeing Holden and listening to him taunt me for the past few hours while I was fucking stuck at that library.

All I wanted was to go through college quietly. I didn't want this shit.

"Don't scold me for this, Callum," I shouted, my heart pounding against my rib cage and my breath coming out choppier. "You don't know what I had to endure for the past few hours or the past few months before I met you. You don't get to decide how I respond to someone who is threatening me!"

Tears filled my eyes, and I didn't have time to stop them before they began pouring down my cheeks. And as much as I tried to push them away to remain strong and unstoppable, the thought of The Council taking me away from my mate or taking my mate away from me was killing me on the inside.

Callum stepped closer to me, giving me those hard hazel eyes. "I'm trying to protect you, Bria."

"Well, you can't!" I shouted through my tears. "Nobody can. Holden already knew who I was. Thiago already knew that I enrolled in this school within the first couple weeks of me leaving town. Nobody can stop this from happening, no matter how hard they try."

I balled my hands into fists, the tears stopping suddenly. A low growl ripped out of my throat, the guttural sound actually comforting now compared to last night. All day, I had been desperately trying to suppress my wolf.

I didn't want her to come back out and hurt anyone, especially Callum.

But she had to remind me that I wasn't alone anymore. I had her by my side. We might not be able to defeat them alone, but we were stronger together against Thiago and The Council. And I would fight until the very end to protect the people I loved.

Another growl rumbled from my chest, and I stepped closer to Callum. I could feel the blood pumping through every one of my veins, the pressure building in my chest and my thoughts running wild with everything I'd do to Thiago if he touched my mate.

"Mine," I growled and moved closer to Callum.

Thiago wouldn't touch my mate.

I stared up at him, tilted my head, and grasped his chin. "You're mine."

Callum didn't back away or show the slightest ounce of fear in his eyes. I expected him to cower back in fear from the monster that I was slowly becoming, the monster that I didn't want to hold back anymore. But he stood stronger than any man I had met before him.

"You're mine to protect," I said to him, my wolf slowly taking control of me and forcing me to sink the tips of my claws into his throat to hold him in place and make our claim on our mate. "Thiago won't touch you."

"Thiago isn't going to touch *you*," Callum said, easily pulling my hand away from his chin and turning us around to press me against the office door. He pinned me against the wood and grasped my chin this time. "You're not going to put yourself into any more danger, Bria. Do you understand me? Let me deal with Thiago."

"No," I growled, inhaling his sweet scent and working myself up further. "You're mine."

Mine.

Mine.

Mine.

Thiago won't touch him.

My wolf rumbled inside me, the sound of her voice stronger than it was last night in bed. An undeniable urge rushed through my body, and I found my canines ripping through my gums and aching to be inside Callum, my classics professor.

This urge wasn't only my wolf's this time. It was mine.

I wanted this more than I wanted anything in my life.

And I refused to let Callum leave this room without my mark on his neck. He had been waiting for this since he marked me, and tonight, I would finally give it to him because there was no holding back anymore. All we could do now was face The Council.

Fuck The Council.

Nobody liked them anyway.

So, I slammed my hands into his chest and sent him stumbling back a few feet toward his desk. I stepped closer to him, my wolf taking complete control of me and becoming a possessive mess of a monster for him.

Callum placed his hands on the sides of his desk and leaned back, his tan biceps flexing, his hazel eyes flickering gold under his dark-framed glasses that he usually wore during his lectures. "Bria …" he breathed out, his voice softer this time.

He knew what I was about to do.

He wanted it.

"You're mine, Callum," I said, drawing my nose up the side of his neck. "And nobody will take you away from me." Before I could stop myself, I sank my teeth into the side of his neck to claim my mate.

Chapter Forty-One

CALLUM

I shivered.

Pleasure rushed through every part of my body from my neck, where Bria's canines were lodged; to my parted lips, breathing in her lovely scent; to my hands that were now grasping on to her hips so tightly that I thought I would break her.

"Bria," I whispered, her name rolling off my tongue.

It wasn't like a feeling that I ever experienced before. It was so much better than the stories told down from generation to generation about how a mate's teeth would feel sinking into my neck and how the woman who loved me finally became a part of my being too.

With her canines still buried deep inside me, Bria let out a long sigh and wrapped her arms around my waist to pull me closer. She paused for a moment, as if she didn't want to pull away, then slowly removed her canines from my throat, pulling me tighter.

"I love you," she whispered against the column of my neck. "I love you, Callum."

Another shiver ran up and down my spine. There was a time in my life that I never thought I would hear those words from a mate. I thought that I was doomed and destined to be alone forever. Hearing those words fall so effortlessly off her tongue made happiness gush through every part of me.

Cupping her face, I forced her to look up at me with her golden wolf eyes. I gently brushed some strands of hair off her forehead and tucked them away behind her ears, my heart racing at the thought of my mate not only marking me for the first time, but also ... loving me.

"I love you too, Bria Benton." I kissed her softly on her lips and rested my forehead against hers. "I fucking love you too."

After a few moments, I could feel her wolf becoming rowdy again.

She shifted from foot to foot, pressing her thighs together and whining softly, "Please."

"Please what?" I asked, growing harder by the second from the scent of her salivating cunt drifting through the room.

"Please, complete the bond." She drew her finger up the front of my pants.

"You want me to make love to you?"

"No," she said, cupping my bulge now and stroking it up and down. "I want you to fuck me all night right in your office, on your desk, all over your students' exams. I don't want you to stop, no matter how much I beg of you."

"Bria ..."

She pulled down my zipper and pulled out my cock, letting a wad of spit drip down. "Please. I wanna suck it," she said in a breathy whisper, dropping to her knees and staring up at me with those golden eyes. She took my cock in her smaller hands and placed her lips on the head, sucking it slowly into her mouth. "Mine."

"Yours, baby," I grunted, pulling her hair behind her shoulders to hold it back. "All yours."

She sucked more of me into her mouth, inch by inch, then pulled back out, a bead of pre-cum dripping from the head of my cock and onto her chin. "Mine," she said again, sucking my shaft back into her hot, wet mouth until she was balls fucking deep.

Staring up at me through watery eyes, she gargled on my cock and cupped my balls, more strings of spit dripping from her bottom lip and onto my office floor between us. She bobbed her head back and forth, her throat bulging every couple moments.

When I couldn't take it any longer, I pulled my cock out of her mouth. "Stand up and let me fuck my mate's tight hole."

Bria drew her tongue across her bottom lip and stumbled to her feet. I bent her over my desk and grasped her hips to pull them back. She arched her back and reached behind me to hold on to my bicep.

"Kiss me," she said, lips covered in spit and slobber.

Lining myself up with her entrance, I pushed myself into her and kissed her hard on the mouth, letting my tongue slip between her lips. I thrust my dick in and out of her clenching hole and pulled back, watching the way her pussy lips clung on to my shaft every damn time I tried to pull out of her.

"More," she moaned. "Give me more, Callum."

I buried my face into the crook of her neck and sucked her mark. She threw her head back, her pussy pulsing over and over and over on my dick and her moans getting lost in my office, probably spilling out into the busy hallways too.

But I didn't care anymore.

And I surely didn't regret fucking my first-year student senseless over my office desk, or in my classroom, or later in my bedroom. Bria Benton might've been my student, but she was my mate. I could do what I wanted with her, and nobody would stop me anymore.

Nobody.

"Callum, I'm coming!" she cried, grasping and wrinkling students' exam papers in her fists. She bucked her hips back and forth against mine, her breathing ragged. "Oh God, Professor Lee. Keep going. My pussy is ..." She let out another moan. "Fuck, it's not stopping."

She continued to buck her hips against mine and moan in my

office, her scent becoming stronger by the second. A thick layer of her juices coated my dick, and the more I fucking admired my mate, the more pressure rose inside me.

Now that we were mated completely, I wouldn't feel bad about shoving my cum as deep as possible into Bria's cervix and hoping that, someday soon, her belly would be round with my pups.

I slammed myself into her one last time, stilled while balls deep, and grunted. "Fuck, Bria."

She might not have gotten pregnant tonight, but one day soon, she would.

I would make sure of it.

Chapter Forty-Two

BRIA

"Hey, girl," Jasmine said, plopping down beside Levi and me in lecture the next morning. She tossed her silky brown hair over her shoulder and wiggled her brows at me. "I heard what happened last night."

My cheeks flushed, and I rubbed my sweaty palms together. "You did?"

"Of course!" Jasmine smacked my shoulder. "What do you think this is? Everyone in the entire pack knows that you marked Alpha Lee last night. When an alpha marks someone and vice versa, everyone in the entire pack can feel it."

I scrunched my nose. "You could feel it?"

"Yeah, like sexually," Levi said, wiggling his eyebrows at me.

Jasmine rolled her eyes. "No. There's like a different aura that falls over the land."

"Levi, you really need to find yourself someone." I shook my head. "If Callum heard you—"

"He'd probably rip my balls off."

Leaning closer to me, Jasmine grabbed my hand. "You know

what this means though?! Soon, you'll be having pups and having a cute little alpha family to raise in our pack. You don't know how excited I am for it!"

"Pups?" I whispered.

"Oh, yeah, Alpha Lee is definitely going to want a family soon. His time is running out."

Jasmine rolled her eyes. "It's not running out, Levi. He's just ... older."

"Much older," I whispered, staring at my desk with my stomach clenched.

Did this mean that Callum wanted to have a family soon? I mean, from those smutty wolf stories that I read online, I kinda gathered that wolf couples liked to reproduce more often than humans. But did that happen in real life too? And by what Callum was saying the other day in his home office to me ...

He definitely wanted pups.

But soon?

"You have to get strong before then though," Jasmine said. "And you could probably guess who asked me to start training with you tonight. Yep, that's right—Alpha Lee because he *definitely* wants to put pups inside you soon."

"God, I think Levi is rubbing off on you a bit, Jasmine," I said, trying to laugh it off.

But I was scared shitless. Pups ... now?!

"Bria getting stronger? I don't even think it's possible," Levi said, tapping his fingers on the desk and shaking his head. He glanced over at me and raised his brows. "I mean, do *you*? Remember a couple days ago, when you literally smashed your finger in the doorframe and walked away like it didn't hurt like a bitch?"

I rolled my eyes and turned back toward my textbook, flipping through it aimlessly.

Jasmine smacked him on the back of the head. "Will you shut your mouth?"

"No, but I'm being serious," Levi continued, staring at the

empty podium, where Callum would show up at any moment. "Like, how the hell are you supposed to get any stronger than you are now? You stopped two alphas from killing each other in your human form the other day."

"Yeah, I guess so." Still, I wouldn't be able to stop Thiago and The Council.

Glancing over Jasmine, I stared at the empty seat beside her. Holden wasn't here yet.

And while I hoped that he would never show his stupid, ugly face in this classroom again, I knew that he would turn up sooner or later—probably sooner along with the rest of The Council.

My stomach tightened as I thought back to yesterday at the library. Between Holden's eyes changing colors even though everyone thought he was human, to his lies, to the way he wanted to know everything about me, something felt terribly wrong.

And it was more than him being in The Council.

Something else was up that I couldn't quite put my finger on yet.

When the door opened in the back of the class, I sucked in a sharp breath and inhaled Callum's calming scent. I glanced over my shoulder. He walked down the center aisle toward the front of the room with his laptop case slung over his shoulder and his eyes on me. I swallowed hard, my cheeks flushing at the thought of yesterday in his office, and glanced at his neck.

While his button-up shirt covered it slightly, I still saw one of my canine marks peeking out from under the material. I pressed my thighs together, wanting nothing more than to jump on him right here and right now.

Ever since last night, I had to hold myself back. Not because I feared my wolf anymore, but because if given the chance, I would ride my professor all night long. And neither one of us would've gotten any sleep for today.

"I want to see you after class, Bria." Callum's voice rang out through my head.

This must've been the mind link.

Last night, Callum mentioned that it formed fully once both wolves marked each other.

I sat up a bit taller, my nipples pressing hard against my T-shirt. I might've *forgotten* to wear a bra today because I wanted to see Callum riled up during class. I wanted him to loosen his tie, pull on his collar, and show me his mark.

"So, that was your plan," Callum said, pulling on his collar and showing me a bit more of my mark. *"You wanted to see this?"*

Sucking in a sharp breath, I pressed my lips together. *"You can hear* my *thoughts?"*

His lips curled into a small smirk, and he walked around the podium, placing his computer case on the table beside him and pulling out his laptop to start the lecture for today. He glanced up at me with those golden eyes and drew his tongue across his lower lip.

"You're a tease, Bria Benton."

My lips curled into a smile. *"Only for you, Professor."*

When the door opened in the back of the classroom again, I sucked in another sharp breath and glanced over at the empty seat next to Jasmine, reserved for Holden. My stomach turned and twisted, and I gripped the seat handles, not daring to look over my shoulder.

Because I knew that if Holden did come to class today, he wasn't coming alone.

Chapter Forty-Three

CALLUM

Thank the Goddess.

Holden didn't show for my class today. I waited for the entire hour for him to waltz in and interrupt me, glare at me from across the classroom like he knew all my secrets, and spill the wolf secret to the humans around us.

I didn't expect anything less from a Council member. Everyone knew that once a human found out about wolves—even if he or she was mated to one—The Council required us to kill them before they shifted or told someone else.

And, fuck, if the entire class found out, that would be a lot of blood on my pack's hands. We would need to take care of them somehow because one of them would be bound to spill our secrets to the entire world.

Bria was different though. She always had been. Even my pack members recognized it.

After I dismissed class, Bria stayed behind while Jasmine and Levi lingered by the door. I wasn't taking any more chances, not with Holden walking around this campus with that shit-eating grin on his face and those wicked eyes that seemed to look Bria up and down whenever she was around him.

"You're training after school today," I said to her. "I've directed Milo to teach you."

She stared up at me with wide eyes and brushed her fingers over the mark she left on my neck last night. "Will you be there?"

All I wanted to do was lean in closer and kiss her softly, but I noticed Chancellor Wilmar walk into the room.

I quickly moved away from Bria before he could see her touch me and shuffled some papers. "Yes."

"Excuse me, Professor Lee," Chancellor Wilmar said, eyeing Bria. "We need to talk."

Bria sucked in a breath and stepped back, slinging her backpack over her shoulders. "I'll take a look into the mythology book you were suggesting, Professor. See you tomorrow." She gave me a small smile and hurried up the aisle toward the exit.

When she left, I shoved my laptop and papers into my bag and walked with Wilmar to my office, my stomach tight. Something wasn't right. He never came down to my classroom and asked to talk.

"Listen, there is no way to beat around the bush with this, Callum," Chancellor Wilmar said, sitting in one of my office chairs and rubbing a hand over his face. "This morning, I had someone tell me some unsettling news."

My heart pounded in my chest, my wolf on the cusp of taking control.

Chancellor Wilmar never called me out like this. Sure, we had meetings, but never unplanned. He had never shown up in my classroom with this look in his eye and that grimace on his face, like he was about to spill the worst news to me.

And all I could think was that he was about to fire me.

But I couldn't let him. I needed to be on school grounds. Bria wasn't safe here alone.

"What is it?" I asked.

"There is a rumor going around that you've been messing around with one of your students—Bria Benton."

Chancellor Wilmar refused to even look me in the eyes, and I was glad that he didn't because my wolf had nearly claimed control of my body. Someone fucking snitched, and I already knew exactly who it was.

"If this rumor is true, Callum, I'm going to have to let you go."

While I hated lying about my mate, this was the only way I could protect us.

I balled my hands into fists behind my back, plastered a confused look on my face, and said, "Bria Benton? She's just one of my students, Chancellor Wilmar. Sure, she stays after class some days and shows up to office hours, but that's because she's very passionate about mythology and Classics class."

Chancellor Wilmar eyed me. "And you haven't touched her?"

Fake a fucking laugh, Callum. Lie. Protect her.

"You know I would never do something like that. I would never risk this job and teaching the subjects that I love by touching one of my students, never mind having a relationship with one of them. I take my job very seriously, Chancellor."

After a couple moments, Chancellor Wilmar swallowed anxiously and nodded. "That's exactly what I thought, Callum. I just needed to confirm it. I can't have anything like that going on in my school. It would give us a bad reputation."

"If you don't mind me asking," I said, trying to be as inconspicuous as possible, "who told you that I was doing something like that? Spreading rumors like this should not go unpunished. This could've cost me my job."

Standing up, Chancellor Wilmar walked to my office door and clasped his hands in front of him as I followed him. "One of your students, who transferred out of your class this morning, reported that you have been paying special attention to Bria Benton. But"—he placed a hand on my shoulder and squeezed—"don't worry about it. I'll get it handled."

My claws sank into my palms behind my back. That fucking asshole.

Holden had been on my shit list since I met him, but now, I was going to kill him.

I would spend the rest of the day searching for him lurking in these school halls. I would not lose my job and Bria because of a scheming Council member. I would not fucking let him leave this university alive.

Chapter Forty-Four

BRIA

Glancing among the warriors training on a cleared field in the forest, I looked for Callum. I hadn't seen him since this morning when the chancellor pulled him away to talk. From the moment I saw the chancellor standing at the door, I knew something wasn't right.

And now that Callum hadn't even tried to contact me since class, I was worried.

What if something had happened to him? What if the chancellor found out about Professor Lee's and my little sexcapades in the classroom, in his office, and even in his bed? What if he had spent all day clearing his office because the chancellor fired him?

My stomach twisted and turned.

But then Callum would've come back to his pack, wouldn't he? He wasn't here.

"We're going to start with a run around the property," Milo said, gaze focused on me. Though he hadn't said merely a couple words to me after Callum marked me, Milo actually gave me a warm-ish smile

—if I could even call it that—and nodded to the woods. "Try to keep up, pup."

The entire pack began at a quick pace, sprinting through the thick brush that surrounded Callum's pack house. My wolf stirred inside me, pushing me faster than even I expected, faster than I had even run before.

"Run faster than him," my wolf said through my mind.

I ignored her and kept a steady pace beside Jasmine and Levi, scanning the woods to check if Callum was here somewhere, watching us. Yet still, there was no sign of him. Jasmine told me not to worry about him, but how could I not?

He wore my mark.

Our mark.

He was mine now, as I was his.

And this whole wolf thing was screwing with my head. I had never once felt the strength of the connection that I had with Callum with anyone else in my life. Not my brother. Not my parents. Not even Adan when we were together.

It was surreal, what being mated did to someone.

After our run around the property, I slowed to a jog once we made it to the field and placed my hands on my knees to *try* to catch my breath. Callum wasn't kidding when he said that this whole training thing would be hard.

We had barely even warmed up yet, and I was already dying.

"You know the drill," Milo said to the rest of the warriors, walking over to me. "Callum has given me orders to teach you how to fight, Bria. If you're going to be our luna and fight The Council, then you're going to know not only how to protect yourself, but also how to kill."

Levi chuckled. "She already kills that dic—"

Jasmine punched Levi square in the jaw to shut him up and pulled him to the side. "I'll take care of Levi while you teach Bria—unless you need us to help you, Beta Milo."

"Go ahead," Milo said to her.

Once Jasmine dragged Levi to the corner of the training field—where warriors were throwing, tossing, slamming into each other with their entire might—Milo turned to me and nodded. "Callum said you're stronger than other humans turned wolves. Can you shift yet?"

Chewing on the inside of my cheek, I shook my head. "No."

"Why don't you try it?" he asked me, lowering down onto his hands and knees and expecting me to do the same.

Reluctantly, I knelt before him and placed my palms on the solid ground, mirroring his steps. When he slowly started to shift into his giant brown wolf, I watched in amazement. I had seen it before, but I didn't know how my body would *ever* do something like that.

"Shift," my wolf said, *"now."*

After taking a steady breath, I squeezed my eyes closed and tried hard to imagine myself turning into a wolf, my nose lengthening into a snout, my teeth growing into canines, my bones breaking and forming into the longer, thicker ones of a wolf.

I spent five minutes desperately trying to shift, only to come up with nothing.

When Milo had enough of me screwing around, he stood and nodded for me to follow him. "It looks like you still need some work. Let's focus on getting you stronger and fighting in your human form. It will help you once you can shift."

Letting out a sigh of disappointment, I stood to my feet and stared up at him. "Okay." I glanced around again to check if Callum was back, but still, nothing. My stomach twisted into knots. "Do you know when Callum will be back? I haven't spoken to him all day."

"He should be back shortly," Milo said. "Now, why don't we start with a fighting stance?"

Scratching the back of my neck, I slowly got down into the best fighting stance I could muster. Truth was that I sucked at this, yet somehow, my body seemed to react the way I needed it to when there was danger around.

Like it had when Callum and Adan were fighting ruthlessly with each other.

Like it had when Holden threatened me.

I hadn't thought. I reacted.

Milo took one look at me and chuckled. "Oh, Bria, this is going to be a long night."

Chapter Forty-Five

CALLUM

One Alpha.

I told Bria that I tried hard to lead like him—with authority and respect—but I lied.

I stared down at Holden lying on my desk, his body covered in deep claw marks and his clothes soaked in blood. With drenched hands, I picked up his carcass and handed it to Adan, who snatched him from me and scrunched up his nose.

"Get him out of my office before someone spots him here," I said.

"You owe me," he said, then glanced out the door crack and sprinted down the hallway.

After I slammed my office door, I ran a blood-covered hand through my hair and swept all the ruined exams and papers off my desk and into a trash bag, cleaning my school office as well as I could before someone saw.

I was no One Alpha. I was an alpha who would do anything to protect his mate.

Even kill.

Once everything was clean, I ran my hands through my hair and paced back and forth in my office, glancing out the window to see Adan disappear into the forest. My stomach was in knots, and I couldn't stop but think that after this, The Council was bound to come find us.

Ten minutes passed, and Adan emerged from the woods. I grabbed my things to bring home and locked up my office to meet him right outside the building. He nodded and grimaced.

"Did you hide his body?" I asked Adan.

"Yes."

"Where?"

Adan growled, "You don't want to know. Drop it. It's done."

After a couple moments, I sighed and ran a hand over my face. I closed the door behind me and walked down the pathway toward the woods with Adan. I didn't like the man, but I didn't want anyone else finding out what I had done.

It felt dirty. It felt filthy. It felt right.

It didn't matter who Holden might've been. All that mattered was that he tried endlessly to take my Bria away from me. He offered her to be with The Council after everything they had done to her. He had trapped her in the library. He had tried to get me fired.

Now, he was gone, and I could finally go home to Bria.

As much as I fucking loathed Adan, I sucked in a breath. "Thanks."

"Thanks?" Adan asked, surprise laced in his voice.

"For taking care of him," I said, balling my hands. "The chancellor asked about my relationship with Bria today. Holden had tipped him off. If I hadn't taken care of him now, then I wouldn't have put it past him to spill the wolf secret to the world next."

"That's the shit that The Council does," Adan said.

We continued down the path toward my pack house in silence.

I couldn't wait to get back to see Bria. I had to ignore her all day because all the professors and the chancellor were watching me closely. Wilmar might've taken my story as truth, but I wasn't taking any chances.

If he even saw me look at Bria on the quad, he might fire me.

She had been contacting me all day, but I had to ignore her.

It hurt me too, so fucking badly. I wanted to scoop her up into my arms, bury my face into the crook of her neck, and kiss the mark I had left on her pretty throat. She was the only woman who could calm me with a touch, with a mere smell.

Walking closer to my property with Adan, I smelled the air to see if I could catch her scent, but my wolf suddenly went wild inside my body and forced me to stop in my tracks. I lifted my nose to the air again, inhaled deeper, and tensed.

A foul scent, mixed with blood, lingered heavily in the air, coasting in from the south—from my property—in waves, curling around all the trees and consuming me. Almost immediately, I shifted into my wolf, my claws digging into the dirt and my canines dripping with saliva.

The Council.

The Council was here.

The Council was trying to take *my* Bria.

Chapter Forty-Six

BRIA

Fire raged around me, engulfing the trees and Callum's people. Screams from the pack echoed through the smoky forest. I pumped my legs as hard as I could and glared into the fire to see if anyone was trapped.

The Council was here for me.

I should've been running far away from here.

But I couldn't get myself to leave while there were innocent people burning in the woods, all because The Council didn't care who lived and who died in war. They would search the ends of this fucking earth until they captured me again.

Still, the promise of horrors and terror forced me to keep moving. I could've turned myself in and stopped this entire thing, but they would do worse to me this time compared to what they had done last time.

Callum didn't know half the shit they put me through, and I refused to ever tell him. If he found out about it, he would hate me for who they had forced me to become, the tests they promised to run, the sterilization.

All for what? I didn't know.

"Please, someone help me!" Callum's mother shouted from the fire.

Digging my heels into the ground, I stopped in my tracks and raced toward her. She was half-shifted, her arm stuck underneath a burning and collapsed tree. I swallowed hard, told myself that I would do anything to protect them, and shoved my hands right onto the burning tree to push it off her.

Sweat dripped down my body from the sheer temperature. I pulled her away from the fire and placed my hands on her wolf-like arm, patting out the flames as best I could, but the damage had already been done to her—these burns would never heal.

Not even as a wolf.

"Dear," she said, fully shifting back into her human form. She clutched her broken and fragile arm and let a tear fall down her cheek. "Your hands—they must be burning. Where did you get all that strength?"

I turned my hands up and stared down at the burn wounds that were healing quickly on my skin—something that had never happened before. If I was still a human, I would've had burns on my hands for the rest of my life.

Even as a werewolf, I didn't think I'd be able to heal this quickly.

Neither did she, apparently.

"Your wounds too," she said in a breathy whisper, staring at my hands with wide eyes.

I glanced down at her with furrowed brows, then shook my head and grabbed her un-broken hand. Fire crackled all around us, and the sound of howling echoed through the woods. Still, I didn't recognize any of the howls as Callum's.

"We have to get out of here. They're coming."

"I can't move," she said, tears pouring down her cheeks. She pulled her hand from mine and ran it across her leg, which was bruising harshly from her knee down. "My leg—I think it's broken. You have to go without me. They're coming for you, not me."

"No," I said, scooping her in my arms. "I'm not leaving you here."

Suddenly, a wolf with large gash wounds across his abdomen sprinted through the forest toward us. With his tail on fire, Milo shifted into his human and grabbed Mrs. Lee from my hold. "We have to get you out of here, Bria. They're pushing us back farther onto our property."

"Where's Callum?" I asked, following him through the trees.

"I saw him back there in the fight. I haven't had a chance to ta—"

I turned on my heel and hurried back toward the fire and the fight. It was so stupid, but I physically couldn't stop myself. I should've known better, but Thiago and The Council would kill Callum, and I couldn't let that happen.

Not when Callum made me the happiest that I'd ever been.

Milo captured my wrist and yanked me back. "We have to—"

Large, vicious wolves leaped over the fire from all directions and stalked toward us with their sharp canines dripping with thick, bloodied saliva. My heart hammered inside my chest as I scurried back until my back hit Milo's bare chest.

Fuck, we're screwed.

"You need to shift, Bria," Milo said, holding Mrs. Lee close to his chest. "That's the only way you're going to get out of here alive. I don't care how hard it is. Fucking shift now! Don't let them kill you."

Adrenaline rushed through my body. I dropped to my knees and squeezed my eyes closed, knowing that I wasn't ready, knowing that I wouldn't be able to shift right here and right now. I didn't have the power or the time.

Still, I tried, and I tried hard.

"Bria!" Milo shouted, placing Mrs. Lee beside me. "Anytime now!"

Tears built up in my eyes, and I tensed my entire body, hoping that I could force myself to shift in front of the entire Council. But deep down, I knew that I wouldn't be able to do anything. I wouldn't be able to see Callum again. I wouldn't get to tell him I loved him either.

When Milo shifted beside me, the world turned to chaos. Wolves leaped at us from all directions. The fire somehow burned even hotter. My heart pounded inside my chest. And I couldn't even get my wolf to come out now.

Yesterday, I tried so hard to suppress her. Now, she wouldn't help me.

Indescribable pain shot through my body.

"Find mate," she whispered in the back of my mind. *"Find mate now."*

My body suddenly started shifting at the feel of pain shooting through my body, which wasn't my pain, but maybe it was Callum's. Had one of the members hurt him? Was that why I could barely feel my fingers?

Before I could shift fully, three Council members piled on top of me, pinned me to the ground, and restrained me completely, their teeth sinking into my flesh. I glanced around to see Milo knocked unconscious on the ground in his human form again with five wolves standing over him and one wolf looming over Callum's mother.

The wolves dragged me through the forest along with them.

I kicked. I screamed. I desperately tried to get away from them.

"Callum!" I shouted through my tears, my vision slowly fading from the sudden depletion of blood from their canine wounds. "Callum, please, help us!"

Chapter Forty-Seven

CALLUM

Amid the fire and fight, I picked up Bria's scent. I killed The Council member in front of me and raced through the woods and warring packs, desperate to find her finally.

"Alpha," Jasmine called from the woods, clutching her waist and stumbling through the trees toward me. Blood gushed from her wound and poured down her chin from her bloody nose. She lifted an arm and pointed behind her. "Bria went that way."

"Get to the hospital," I said, hurrying past her and toward the direction she had pointed.

I sniffed the air and picked her scent back up. My legs moved faster than even I could keep up with, and I transformed into my beast to run even faster because she couldn't be gone. I wouldn't fucking allow those bastards to take her.

But the faster I moved, the less and less Council members got in my way. They were running back, retreating almost. My wolves waited for my orders, and I found myself stopping at the outskirts of the fire.

"They're clearing out," one of my warriors said through the mind link.

But The Council didn't retreat. They retrieved what they came for.

They fucking had my Bria.

"Follow them," I ordered, racing through the woods along the fire and passing all my wounded warriors and pack mates. My chest tightened at the sight of how many of my people they had either killed or gravely injured in the past ten minutes.

Adan was right.

The Council was shit. Fucking shit.

"The fire is too thick," another wolf said through the mind link. *"It goes on for miles."*

I froze in my spot, an undeniable rage rushing through my body, and glared at the fire in front of me that seemed to grow even wilder all of a sudden. My hands were covered in blood; my body felt like it was engulfed in flames itself.

She couldn't be gone.

Forty-three fucking years. Forty-three years.

I'd waited for so damn long to be with her.

Even if I tried to fight through the flames, I didn't think I would make it. We needed to put them out, regroup, and get our most skilled trackers out on the hunt for The Council and Bria. Adan must've had an idea of where they were headed.

But I hated the thought of leaving Bria with them. Even for a couple moments.

"Find your way to the pack house," I said through the mind link to my entire pack, my hands balling into fists by my sides and my heart clenching. *"We need to regroup, heal those who are hurt, and figure out a plan."*

"What about mate?" my wolf asked me. *"We need to find her."*

If The Council had her, they would be long gone by now. They wouldn't stick around and wait for us to put out the fire. They could be hours away from us once we finally cleared the forest of flames and smoke.

That was what they were banking on too.

I wouldn't let my pack members blindly run into a war that we would lose.

Fuck. I ran a hand through my wild hair, pushing back the tears to be strong for my pack. *I'm coming back for you, Bria. I won't let them have you. I'll find you and kill them all. Every last one of them.*

After helping the wounded wolves, I took one glance around the part of the forest that wasn't burning for any survivors, then hurried back to the pack house to see who had made it and who hadn't. Did they capture anyone else other than Bria?

When I reached the living room, I scanned the room and clenched my jaw. "Where's Milo? My mother?" I asked Jasmine and Levi, who lay back on the couch with half his face swollen. "Why aren't they here?"

Levi frowned and glanced over at Jasmine, who stared at the ground with tears in her eyes.

She doubled over into Levi's shoulder and cried against him, shaking her head from side to side. "I wish I were stronger. I heard them screaming for help on the other side of the flames earlier. I couldn't do anything."

Instead of pushing her away, Levi enveloped Jasmine into a hug. I clenched my jaw and hurried through the house, desperate to find them somewhere upstairs, maybe in the library or my bedroom, the bathroom, somewhere.

But they weren't here.

Mom, Milo, and my mate were all gone.

The Council took them from me.

And I vowed to get them back. Even if it killed me.

Chapter Forty-Eight

BRIA

When I woke up, my head rested in Mrs. Lee's lap. I blinked my eyes open and stared up at the woman who looked like she had been beaten and tortured for the past day by The Council. I didn't know how much time had passed, but she looked so bad.

All because of me.

"Where are we?" I whispered, my voice hoarse and my throat dry.

I hesitantly sat up and held a hand to my head, grunting. Milo sat in the corner of a cell with his head against a stone wall and his body stripped of all clothes. His skin was coated in a thin layer of dried blood.

"In their prison," Milo said.

Chest tightening, I glanced over at Mrs. Lee, who had tears on her cheeks.

"My son has been waiting for you for years," she said, a tear sliding down her wrinkled face. She gently grasped my hand with her trembling one. "That first day he saw you, he came home with a huge smile on his face. I have never seen him that happy before."

Everything seemed so disoriented. I didn't know what was happening or where this was coming from. We should've been trying to escape, not talking about the stories of Callum and the pack. Though ... just hearing his name made me sad.

"When they come back, find a way to escape." Mrs. Lee smiled strongly at me despite half her body being broken and the gashes all over her flesh. She was stronger than I ever hoped to be. "I'll hold them off the best I can."

And while Callum hadn't really taught me much about pack dynamics yet, his mother was willing to die for me. She wanted to sacrifice herself, so the new luna of her pack and her son's mate would survive.

But I wouldn't let that happen. She could barely move.

"No," I said, pulling my hands out of hers and standing. I stormed over to the cell bars. "We're getting out of here."

"Don't touch the bars," Beta Milo said from the corner, his right eye swollen shut and his busted lip bloody and bruising. "They're solid silver and will sear your skin right off, Bria. Silver is especially dangerous to humans becoming wolves, as they don't know how to handle the pain."

Milo might've told me not to touch the silver, but I couldn't sit in this cell with Beta Milo and Callum's aging mother. We wouldn't survive here like this through the night. I'd seen and heard the terrors of what The Council did to people during the night.

I refused to let that be us—or at least, I refused to let that be them.

If I had to stay here to please Thiago and have him torture me day in and day out, just to ensure that my mate's pack was protected, then I would. Nobody deserved to die because of me, especially because The Council couldn't care less about Callum and his wolves.

They wanted me. They found me. They had me.

Everyone else would be useless to them.

After taking a deep breath, I grasped the silver bars and ignored the searing pain that shot through my body. Milo shot up from the ground, wrapped his arms around my stomach, and tried to pull me away.

But I refused to let go.

I held on to the bars for dear life and used all the damn strength I had left inside me to pull them apart, literally forcing them away to create a space big enough for even Milo to slip through and escape.

Once the space was large enough with some wiggle room, I dropped my hands from the bars and relaxed in Milo's arms, my chest rising and falling and hot tears welling up in my eyes, threatening to fall from the sheer pain of silver.

"What's wrong with you?" Milo asked, letting me down gently.

While his question might've been full of anger and spite, his voice wasn't filled with annoyance, but instead, it was filled with wonder. He glanced at the silver bars, shock on every part of his face, and let me go for a second. When his hands left my waist, my knees gave out, and I collapsed.

Before I could fall to the ground, Milo caught me and helped me to my feet.

"We have to go," I said once I regained my balance.

"But you—"

"I'm fine." I pushed him away and toward Callum's mother. "Carry her. You won't be able to carry us both and get out of here alive. I'll run beside you. But it's important to me that you get her to safety yourself."

"You'd better follow me," Milo said, scooping Mrs. Lee in his arms. "If Callum finds out that I left his mate here and brought only his mother home, then he will kill everyone in his path. He's been waiting for you for far too many years."

My stomach twisted because I knew we all wouldn't make it out of here alive. I had slipped through The Council's fingers once. They would not let me escape another time. But I needed to buy enough time for us to get as far away as possible.

I needed Milo and Mrs. Lee to escape.

Not for the sake of my conscience, but for Callum.

"I'll be right behind you. Don't look back. Just keep running," I said.

After glancing out of the cell, Milo stepped out with Callum's mother, sniffed the air, and hurried down the left corridor, propelling himself forward quicker than he had during our run mere hours earlier.

Even though I told him not to look back, he glanced over his shoulder to make sure I was running after him. I pumped my legs as quickly as I could, though I was still so much slower than a wolf who was even in human form and carrying someone else.

The hallways and passages were all underground, and I swore we ran around them multiple times, unable to figure out how to get out. There was barely any light besides a couple flickering torches down here.

"A door," I whispered. "Up ahead. Go through it."

"Are you sure?" Milo asked.

"There looks to be light from underneath it. Go."

Though I wasn't sure in the slightest.

Still, Milo sprinted ahead, ripped the door open, and stared out into a dark pathway that led out of this building.

But as we were about to escape, Thiago captured me by the waist from behind and pulled me away from Milo. "Oh, you're not going anywhere, Bria Benton. You've gotten away from me once. I won't let you go again."

Chapter Forty-Nine

BRIA

With Callum's mother in his arms, Beta Milo stopped in the middle of the lawn, about to escape, and turned around to face me. I struggled in Thiago's grip, desperately trying to get away even though I knew it was useless.

From the moment I woke up in the cell, I knew I wouldn't be able to leave.

Especially not this easily.

"Go!" I shouted at them, hearing the other warriors running down the steps toward us.

If they made it down here, then they would torture Milo and Callum's mother. And I couldn't live with myself to see them hurt *or* hurting. It was all my fault that they were here. It was my fault that they were captured and in pain.

I couldn't let anyone else be punished for my wrongdoings.

Beta Milo placed Callum's mother down on the lawn, growling and about to shift. I balled my hands into fists, being dragged backward and farther into the building by Thiago.

"Don't fight!" I growled at him. "Leave! Get her to safety! Now!"

For a moment, Beta Milo tried to shift into his wolf, but it almost looked like he couldn't, or his wolf was fighting himself. I didn't quite understand what was happening. Beta Milo was stubborn as hell, almost as much as Callum.

If he wanted to shift into his wolf, he would.

Still, he struggled against his wolf, finally succumbing to the thought that he couldn't, and scooped Callum's mother up into his arms, turning his back toward me and running through the woods before the other warriors could come out.

When he disappeared from my sight, I finally stopped struggling. Thiago held on to me for a moment longer, then finally let me go, his hands slipping from my waist and his intense gaze focused on me.

I didn't have to turn around to face him to see it. I could fucking feel it.

"You did good," he said to me. "That was believable."

My stomach turned, and I glanced down at my feet, feeling nothing but guilt running through my veins. Tears welled up in my eyes, and I lifted my head slightly to stare emptily into the woods.

The warriors continued to pour down the stairs until they surrounded Thiago and me. I raised my hand before they could run out into the woods and capture Milo and Callum's mother. Nobody else deserved to die.

"Promise me that they'll be safe," I said through gritted teeth, tears spilling down my cheeks. "Promise me that you'll put out the fire you started at their pack and use the medicine you have to heal their wolves, so none of them die."

"That was the deal," Thiago said to me. "But if they're already dead, then we ca—"

I twirled on my heel, glared up at Thiago, and poked a hard finger into his chest. "No, you're going to save them all. I know you have medicine here to save even the recently deceased. You will save them, or you won't get anything from me."

Rage rushed through me, and Thiago's face paled.

"I know what you want from me. Holden was crystal clear

during our chat in the library, where I knew you were watching. If you don't keep up your side of the bargain, we have no deal, Thiago."

"That deal was made before your mate murdered Holden."

I clenched my twitching jaw and snatched Thiago's throat in my hand, shoving him against the wall so hard that his body dented the stone. "You're going to heal them, and then you get everything you've been torturing me over for the past two years. No more deals with my family. You have a deal with me now."

And while I was doing this to save Callum and his pack, I still felt guilt deep in my bones, rushing through my veins, spreading throughout my entire being.

This wasn't how my life was meant to turn out, and if Callum knew ...

He would hate me.

When I let go of his throat, he turned to the warriors behind him. "Send them supplies."

"But, Alpha—"

"Now," he growled, rubbing his neck.

A couple of warriors disappeared into another room and came out a few moments later with advanced supplies, heading toward Callum's pack.

Before they could exit through the door, I placed my hand up to block them. "Put out the fire too."

They glanced at Thiago.

"Do it," Thiago ordered.

Once I pulled my arm away, they scurried out the back door to travel to Callum's property. I turned back to Thiago, loathing myself and what I had become since Callum marked me. I fucking loved being with him. I just hated being hunted like this.

I hated putting people in danger.

"That wasn't how we agreed it'd go down," I said through gritted teeth, pushing back the tears because I didn't want him to think I was weak. Thiago took advantage of the weak. "You promised me that nobody would get hurt."

"You didn't give us much of a choice with your power."

"You have scientifically advanced wolves," I ground out to him. "You could've done it cleaner. You could've captured me without anyone getting hurt or dying in the process. But you wanted to show how much power you had."

But he didn't know true power. Yet.

He wouldn't know true power until I gave it to him.

That was the deal.

This power building inside me in exchange for never hunting me or Callum's pack again. And I had not wanted to be hunted or hurt for the majority of my life. It was a deal that I couldn't pass up, no matter how terrible the consequences were.

I wanted this endless torture to end.

Chapter Fifty

CALLUM

Forty minutes after I gathered all the people gravely injured from the attack into the pack house, I stood at the door and watched impatiently as the pack doctors healed them. Most of my pack warriors were down for the count, which meant we wouldn't have a strong pack to find and attack The Council.

Even Adan's pack was injured.

Beta Milo thrust open the door behind me, holding Mom in his arms. My eyes widened, and I took my mother from him and placed her on a bed next to other warriors, so she could be healed.

When I knew she was settled, I glanced out the door to find Bria. "Where is she? Where's Bria?" I asked Milo.

Beta Milo looked away and refused to make eye contact with me. My stomach turned and twisted, and I balled my hands into fists so tightly that my claws sank right through the skin on my palms.

"I tried to stay," Beta Milo reasoned, head hung down in guilt. "I tried so fucking hard. You can ask your mother. I wanted to shift and run after her, capture her from Thiago and bring her with us. But ..."

"But what?" I growled, anger rushing through me. "But you didn't bring your luna home."

Milo was the beta of this fucking pack, and Bria was a new wolf, who hadn't even shifted yet. She couldn't protect herself there with him. I had seen the fear in her eyes every fucking time she spoke about him. There was more than what she told me.

He had done or promised unspeakable things to her.

"I'm sorry." Beta Milo bowed his head for the first time ever. "She ordered me to leave."

"He's telling the truth," Mom said, shaking her head. "I wanted to save her, too, but as soon as those words left her mouth ... Goddess, it sounded and felt like an alpha's order. Stronger than any orders you've ever given."

Whispers erupted throughout the pack house, and I growled to silence my pack and my family. I stared at Mom and Beta Milo, my chest in tight knots. How could Bria's command be as strong as an alpha command? How could she—

"One Alpha," Mom said, giving me a smile. "It's her."

"It can't be," I said. "It's a fable."

"You're a mythology professor, Callum," Mom said. "You know that many of those stories come from the truth. And I know that you believe in him—or her—too, no matter how much you think you don't. She's real, and she's Bria."

"Alpha, the fire went out," one of my warriors said, hurrying into the room.

Another wolf came from behind him with duffel bags. He dropped them in front of me and unzipped them. "There is medication here, too, for all our wounded wolves. We found it on the outskirts of our property."

"It's Bria. I'm sure of it." Mom smiled wider. "She pulled the silver bars apart with her bare hands. It was unbelievable what she could do, even as part werewolf now. If she didn't have One Alpha's power, then she wouldn't have been able to do that. At all."

"She's not even a wolf yet," I said, pacing back and forth. "Why would they want her?"

Mom pressed her lips together and stared at me through wide and watery eyes, then glanced over at Beta Milo, who looked down at his feet and clenched his jaw. "You know why they want her. Thiago desires power. He will do anything to take it from her."

Unable to stop myself, I let out a growl and stormed upstairs, leaving my pack alone. I hurried up to my office, pushing a hand through my thick brown hair, and slammed the door behind me. Pain rushed through every bit of my being, my chest tightening until I could barely breathe.

Why hadn't I told Bria I loved her today?

Why had I ignored her? Why didn't I protect her? Why was she gone?

If I had been a bit quicker or more on my toes or smarter, I could've stopped this before The Council descended upon my pack, started a raging fire, and stole my mate, the one woman I had been searching for my entire life.

Anger overtaking me, I slammed my fist right through the drywall, threw the bookcase to the other side of the room, and ripped the important papers off my desk.

What the fuck was wrong with me? Why had I let this fucking happen?!

A ferocious roar escaped my throat as I continued to tear my office to pieces. This was my fucking fault. I couldn't be strong enough. I couldn't save her. Thiago and his asshole warriors marched onto *my* property and stole *my* mate.

The One Alpha book lay at my feet, staring up at me and taunting me. All my life, I had looked up to the man in this book. I had dedicated years of my life to try to be like him, but when the time came, I couldn't lead like this.

I kicked the book across the room and watched it slam against the wall. "Fuck."

After it slammed, the pages opened up, and a piece of paper

slipped from the inside, landing on the cover of the book once it fell to the ground. It must've been one of Bria's many notes she took on every mythology book I gave her.

My lips turned into a frown, and I stopped ripping up my office and walked over to it, kneeling down in front of the book and taking it in my hands. On the slip of paper, in Bria's cursive handwriting, read the words: *I'm sorry, Callum. I did this to protect us. If you want to hate me, I understand, but I refuse to see you or any of your pack mates die because of this.*

For moments, I stared at the note in confusion. And then it hit me.

Bria planned for her capture. Bria wanted The Council to take her.

She fucking wanted to protect me and our pack when it should've been the other fucking way around. I should've been the one protecting her, saving her from the torture that Thiago would soon put her through, if he hadn't already.

At the bottom of the page, there was an arrow. I turned the paper over and let a tear fall down my cheek, feeling so fucking helpless. My mate fucking sacrificed herself for me after I had waited years for her, after I thought I finally got to keep her.

The rest of the note read: *I'm sorry that it came to this. I'm sorry that I put you in danger. I'm sorry that the next time you see me, I'll be nothing anymore. Not the strong wolf that you marked, maybe not even a wolf. But know that no matter what happens, I will always love you even if you dedicate your life to hunting me down and killing me for this betrayal. You're mine, and a good mate always protects her alpha.*

Chapter Fifty-One

BRIA

Thiago stared at me and followed me toward the doctor's office in the middle of this pack house that was way too large for me to honestly keep it straight. I walked with my shoulders pushed back and my head held high.

"Please, don't do this," my wolf said to me. *"Think about mate."*

Truth was that I wasn't confident that this was the right choice. I knew that being here was the wrong one. I knew that all Thiago wanted was power and domination over the entire world, but ... he promised me that Callum would be taken care of, and he had kept half his promise already.

He had the medication ready and sent it to Callum's pack.

Even before college, Thiago *always* kept his promises. Good or bad.

When we reached the doctor's office, I stopped at the door, reality setting in for the first time today. This was the plan I had made with Holden, but now that I was trapped in this pack house and had traded my life away, I didn't want to be here. I didn't want to give up this part of myself that I was slowly beginning to love—my wolf.

She was everything to Callum.

When I let her go, would he ever love me again? If I took away the one person that he'd been searching for since he turned eighteen, would he forgive me? Would he hunt me down and hate me for trading her?

Did he love me or her?

I balled my hands into fists and let the tears fall down my cheeks, my chest tight. Being here might be the end of me. If Thiago didn't hold up his end of the deal after he took my wolf from me, then I would be helpless.

He could do anything he wanted.

I knew that when I came here. But anything was better than having Callum and his pack hunted down every single day, pack members dying and tortured, all so The Council could find me. What hurt the most was having to lie and betray Callum.

For all of eternity, I would never forgive myself.

Never.

I could only imagine how he felt, reading my note, if he had even found it yet, but I needed him to know that I loved him, no matter what happened. He deserved that much, especially from his mate.

Thiago shoved me into the room. I stumbled toward the chair and sat down, shuffling my feet together against the cold tiled floor. More tears welled up in my eyes, and I refused to look at Thiago.

For the past day, I had gone over and over all the possible outcomes once Thiago had my power. I glanced up at him. He stared at me intently, narrowing his eyes and making sure I wouldn't make a run for it.

"Don't remove One Alpha from her. She keeps it," he said, lips forming a smirk. He walked over to me slowly, stalking around me like I was his prey. "All this time, since I found out that you had it inside you, I thought that I wanted to take it from you. But now, I see that all I have to do is force you into submission, like all my other warriors, brainwash you, make you become subservient to only me. And then I have total control without losing myself."

My heart raced, and I went to stand up to tell him that this wasn't part of the deal, but cuffs suddenly locked my wrists and ankles to the chair, and I couldn't move. Thiago stepped away from me and grabbed a needle hooked up to a monitor with some fluid inside it.

He slipped it into my arm and turned on the machine, pumping fluids into my body.

"You're mine now, Bria Benton. My slave."

Thiago suddenly tensed, eyes glazing over, as if he was talking through the mind link. Callum's eyes had done that when he was chatting with me through our newly formed one, and at that time, I thought it was the most magical thing.

"Stay here," Thiago said, looking at me, then at the doctor, and then rushed toward the door to the office room. "Don't let her leave until the procedure is complete. I have business that I need to handle." Before he walked out the door, he turned to me. "Don't leave, or I'll kill every last one of your pack mates."

And with that, he walked out the door. The dark gray automatic doors closed behind him and locked, the lights across the middle of the door turning a beaming red color. I stared at the door for a couple moments, wanting to leave so badly, then turned back to the doctor.

He stepped toward me with a needle to take a blood sample. I stayed still in the seat and stared emptily at the ground, feeling the prick of the needle and trying hard not to bawl my eyes out. This was the fucking end for me.

For us.

"I don't know why he wants my wolf so badly," I muttered. "I can't even shift."

"You can't shift?" the doctor asked, suddenly stilling. He furrowed his brows and pulled the needle out of my arm, hurrying to one of his little trinkets on the table that did God knew what.

"No. I can't shift," I repeated.

After tapping a button, a green light came on in the machine. He tensed and shook his head, muttering the word, "No," over and over under his breath. In a moment, he turned toward the door and sprinted at it. "Alpha! Wait!"

"What is it?" I asked him.

But he didn't answer me.

My wolf thrashed around inside of me for control, and with the fluids pumping into my system, I was beginning to lose control of myself and my human. I was slipping, so she easily took the power from me.

Using all our strength, she broke the cuffs around my wrists and ankles and stood. I hurried toward the door before the doctor could slip out of it and find Thiago. He scrambled to get away from me, but I stopped him and held him still.

"What did you find?" I growled.

"It shouldn't be possible," he said, shaking his head. "It's not."

"What?" I growled.

"The first sterilization shot we gave you years ago ..." He paused. "It didn't work."

"What do you mean, it didn't work?" I asked, my heart leaping inside my chest.

"I mean, you're not sterile. Not anymore."

If I wasn't sterile, if what he was saying was true, that meant that I was fighting for more than me now. I couldn't sit back and let them take this away from me. If Thiago found out, then he would try to rip out my uterus with his bare hands.

Instead of letting the *poor* doctor go, I wrapped my hands harder around his neck and snapped it until his body fell lifeless in my hands, until he was dead and could never tell Thiago anything. Then, I took control of my wolf and ripped the needle from my arm to stop the fluids.

Because now, I was fighting for Callum and me and maybe ... someone else too.

Chapter Fifty-Two

CALLUM

"Find Bria," my wolf growled, lashing out inside of me to break free from my control. He seized inside my body, throwing and shoving at my insides. *"Find mate now. We need her. We need to protect her."*

I crumpled Bria's note in my hand and cut my claws into the thin paper, fury rushing through my entire being. Teeth lengthening into sharp canines, fingernails extending into deadly claws, my wolf ached for control.

If I gave it to him, he'd make senseless fucking choices. He wasn't in the right mind, but hell, neither was I. Our mate was gone. And I might've known the real reason why she left, but I still couldn't stop thinking about how she left *me*.

After I waited years for her.

My heart was breaking, shattering, fucking destroying me.

Bria left me, and I wasn't doing a thing about it. I was just wallowing in my self-pity.

Someone knocked on my office door, then pushed it open. Mom grasped on to the handle for dear life as she stepped into the room.

Her torso was wrapped in bandages, yet she didn't show a single bit of pain on her face.

She never did.

She closed the door behind her and frowned at me. "Callum."

"She went with them willingly, Mom," I said through gritted teeth, hands balled into tight fists. "She traded her life for our safety because she didn't think we would be able to defeat them. And we couldn't. *I* fucking couldn't."

"Callum," she said, moving closer. "It's not your fault."

"I couldn't protect my mate," I said, my anger fading away and my voice becoming throaty and hoarse. My chest tightened.

If anything happened to her, I would never forgive myself. I would never be able to lead my pack as an alpha, knowing that I let my mate, who I waited decades for, trade her life to protect my people—who she barely knew—and me.

"It's what any caring and worthy luna would do," Mom said.

"She barely even knows anyone or what lunas do. She knows nothing about being a wolf. I haven't taught her enough. I should've drilled it into her. I should've forced her to learn, to train, to be with our pack more often."

Mom smiled. "She doesn't have to know what lunas do or the rules most alphas make their lunas follow, like caring for their pack. Strong lunas lead by example. They do what's right for the group instead of just for her."

I shook my head and cursed underneath my breath, knowing that she was right. Bria must've thought that sacrificing herself was the only way to stop the madness, but still, it didn't feel right. I should've been there tonight, not fucking ignoring her.

She was mine.

She belonged to *me*. Not him.

And I refused to let Thiago torture her for eternity, to take her wolf away from her, to force her to live in fear forever. Bria might've been the luna of this pack, but she was my long-awaited mate. I would get her back even if it killed me.

"But you're the alpha, Callum," Mom said. "Alphas might do anything to protect their pack, but they would also sacrifice everything to protect their mate. Whatever you're planning on doing, know that I support you. I want to do everything in my power to protect you, but I know you'll run off to find her either way. You're my only son. Be safe."

"I will."

Storming out of my destroyed office and to the others gathered downstairs, I faced my pack. They knew that Bria was gone, and they had probably heard me going fucking crazy upstairs, but ... fuck.

Nobody dared to say a word.

"Running to The Council's pack to retrieve Bria is dangerous," I said, clenching my jaw.

Part of me wished that I didn't always lead by example, that I didn't take all those One Alpha lessons to heart, that I forced people to do what I wanted them to do. But I wasn't like Thiago, and maybe that would kill Bria. I would have to fucking live with that shit.

"Thiago's pack won't go easy on us. They'll try to kill us, and they might succeed. If you don't want to come with me, stay back. We've been attacked. I understand that you're wounded, but I'm leaving. I won't let my mate trade her life for us."

After a couple moments of silence, I inhaled sharply, pushed my shoulders back, and walked to the front door to leave my pack behind and find my mate. When I reached the door, I yanked it back with such ferocity, my wolf slowly taking control, that I ripped the door right off its hinges.

"Hey," Beta Milo shouted, following me toward the door along with a group of warriors. "You're not going alone. Bria might not have transformed into a wolf yet, but she's still our luna. She's sacrificed her life for all of us, not just you."

I glanced back at the warriors, catching Jasmine and Levi not bickering for once and standing tall beside Adan's pack warriors, who looked ready for any battle that Thiago could throw at them.

"We're coming too," Jasmine said, glancing over at Levi. "Bria's our friend."

"Me too," Adan said, glancing back at his warriors. "I know the ins and outs of that place. They're lacking security on the northern border. I've snuck in with my warriors many times before to retrieve Bria, medication, and intel. They have a science wing toward the west. And their security room is on the upper level."

After looking back at my warriors, I transformed into my wolf and turned toward the forest, howling to the moon that had risen some time ago. "Then, we run, find Bria, and destroy The Council for good."

Chapter Fifty-Three

BRIA

When the doctor fell lifelessly to the ground, I sprinted toward the door and opened a keypad, hitting random keys and hoping that I would be able to unlock the room somehow. I racked my brain for any sort of code that Thiago would have used.

768

No.

9129

Nothing.

666—because he was the devil himself.

Nada.

Annoyed, I slammed my palm against the keys and hit Enter a bunch of times. I didn't know the code and would never be able to figure it out. While I might've only met Thiago a couple of times, I didn't know shit about him.

Most of the time, Mom and Dad would knock me out while I was here and they were running tests on me. Hell, I didn't even know that I had One Alpha inside of me until I read that book that Callum had.

Thiago and my parents would always mention One Alpha, but I thought it was some type of gene or something. I didn't think it was an actual wolf lingering inside me. How the hell would I put that together?

But now, I wished I had figured it out sooner. I wished that I had found the time to understand Thiago's motivations, snooped into his offices, found *something* that would help me get the fuck out of here.

After searching the doctor for a key card and finding nothing, I paced the room. Back and forth and back and forth until I was nearly ripping my hair out, searching for another way to escape. It was useless.

I sprinted back up to the locked door and threw my body against it, summoning my wolf. My body dented the metal slightly, but it didn't budge. I slammed my body against it again and again, the dent becoming larger and deeper.

On the fifth slam, the door snapped open.

Yet it wasn't because of me.

Thiago stood on the other side of the doorway, eyes a piercing gold and canines extended. He stormed into the room and slammed the door behind him, growling low and deep, trying to intimidate me.

I stepped back, heart pounding inside my chest.

"What the fuck are you doing?" he asked. "And where is my doc—"

He glanced down at the ground, where I had killed his doctor in cold blood, and then he looked at the equipment he was using.

Before he could even use the thousand-dollar equipment, I grabbed a spare part that had fallen to the ground from my initial struggle with the scientist and smashed it to pieces, making sure that the machine wasn't usable in the slightest.

He could never find out those results. Ever.

In one of Callum's books, I read that One Alpha could be passed down from mother or father to child. If Thiago found out about the results, he would rip my womb right out of my body with his claws. He wouldn't care; he wanted the power for himself.

"Get over here, you little bitch." He seethed, stalking closer to me. "You're going to fucking pay for that shit."

I hurled the broken piece of equipment at him, and then my wolf forced me to drop to all fours. She seized control of my body. My bones snapped, the harrowing sound echoing through the entire room. My claws lengthened, my canines extending.

And for the first time, my body transformed into that of a wolf, standing tall in front of Thiago. Fear flashed in his eyes, and he stepped back. I lifted my paw, new and improved senses overcoming me.

But when I went to stalk forward, I stumbled.

Thiago furrowed his brows, then straightened his back and smirked down at me. "It worked."

He chuckled menacingly as I stumbled forward again, my vision blurring.

What was happening? Why couldn't I walk straight?

"You already have the drug in your system," he said. "There's no fighting it. Close your eyes, Bria, and sleep for me. When you awaken, you will be mine for good."

Desperately, I forced my eyes open, blinking the darkness away as much as I could.

But it was consuming me, spreading around my vision, taking control of me. I clenched my jaw and forcefully rubbed my eyes with my paws, hoping that the dark would fade. Still, nothing.

I couldn't see any light.

My fingers were numbing. My limbs tingled. My head was light and fuzzy.

With all my might, I tried to fight the brainwashing chemical that they pumped into me. But the world faded quickly around me, my consciousness succumbing to the darkness and Thiago's evil voice echoing through my head.

Worst of all, I knew I was about to lose consciousness and could do nothing about it.

All I could seem to do was think about Callum, the doctor's test, and how Thiago could never find out the test results ... that the first shot of sterilization didn't work and that I might be pregnant.

Yet if he gained control of me ... he would soon know *everything*.

He would kill my baby, and then he would kill me.

Chapter Fifty-Four

CALLUM

After sneaking onto Thiago's property from the northern border, like Adan suggested, we split into our two packs. Adan was to sneak into the castle and cut the security cameras, destroy any footage of us being there, and kill as many Council members as possible.

We were to head right for the cells and the prison, where they were probably holding Bria.

Once we killed the two guards at the doors, we snuck into the palace and rushed through each of the prison cells, desperately trying to find my mate and the pack's luna. But every cell that we stepped into was empty.

No dead bodies.

No blood.

No Bria.

"Where the fuck is she?" I asked myself, looping around the cells once more and glancing into each one of them, as if I had missed her the first time.

Yet something wasn't clicking for me. This place sounded a bit *too* quiet to house all of The Council members.

"Alpha," one of my warriors said from the door we walked into. "You might want to see this."

Hurrying out the door, I stopped dead in my tracks when I saw Thiago holding Adan—*fucking Adan*—the man who I could barely put a scratch on during our fight, by the scruff of the neck. Beaten and bleeding all over, Adan hung lifelessly in Thiago's arms.

"Adan!" Jasmine screamed, lunging toward him.

I pulled her back, knowing that Thiago would kill her in a moment's notice. She struggled in my hold for a moment, and then Levi seized her body to hold her back.

I stepped toward him and growled, "Let me go and give me Bria."

"I promised Bria that I wouldn't attack you unless provoked," Thiago said. "I'd say that this is a sure reason to kill you now. Don't you think?"

Taking another step forward, I clenched my jaw. "If you fucking touched her, I'll kill you."

"Touched Bria?" Thiago asked. "Me? Never."

"Where the fuck is she?"

"Oh." Thiago chuckled darkly. "I don't think you really want to see what she's become."

"NOW!" I growled, about to lose total fucking control.

"I'll call Bria out, but I'm warning you ... she might not even recognize you or your wolf."

My heart raced, and I balled my hands into fists.

"Bria," Thiago cooed. "Come here."

A midnight-black wolf, almost my size, stalked out from behind him. Canines extended and dripping with saliva and claws digging into the hardening dirt, she glared right at me—her mate—and let out a ferocious growl.

"I can make her play," Thiago taunted, a smirk across his face. "Wanna see?"

After growling at him, I stepped forward. "I will kill you."

"Jump for me, Bria," Thiago said, not once looking at Bria, but keeping his gaze focused on me.

And as he finished his sentence, Bria's enormous wolf leaped high into the air.

Thiago placed his hand on the top of her head. "Good girl."

Another growl clawed its way out of my throat. "Let her go!"

He knelt down and wrapped his arm around her torso, stroking her black fur and whispering something into her ear. When he turned back to me, he smirked. "Bria Benton is now *my* plaything."

My wolf seized control of me, and I leaped forward, running at full speed toward him.

Bria Benton was mine, nobody else's.

Thiago stood up and let go of Bria, nodding toward me. "Attack your mate, Bria. Show him how powerful you truly are."

Chapter Fifty-Five

BRIA

Claws extended, canines aching for flesh, focus solely on Callum, I leaped at my mate.

A carnal rage inside me urged me forward to fight him with everything that I had, to sink my teeth into any bit of flesh that I could, to prove myself, and to kill him. Thiago ordered my wolf to slaughter his, and my wolf craved to do just that.

The world turned to chaos around me, Thiago's warriors fighting Callum's and Adan's. Callum shifted into his wolf and dodged my attacks, one after the other. But I didn't stop moving forward toward him, even when the battlefield reeked of blood.

I couldn't stop.

I wanted to so badly.

"Bria," Callum said through the mind link, but my wolf didn't stop.

We slashed his shoulder, making him bleed out slightly. He healed it quickly and dodged another one of my attacks, ducking underneath my paw. I leaped forward, growling, and snatched his paw between my teeth.

"Stop it."

Callum wasn't fighting as hard as he had during his battle with Adan. He was either already hurt or he didn't want to hurt me. Deep down, I knew it was the latter. He would rather die himself than to see me in pain.

And I couldn't fucking believe that my wolf didn't recognize it—her own mate.

I desperately tried to stop myself, but my wolf wouldn't seize back control from Thiago. He had pumped that fluid into our bloodstream, the same way he had probably done that to his hundreds upon hundreds of warriors before me, and taken complete control.

No matter how hard I tried, I couldn't stop my body or my wolf.

"I'm so scared, Callum," I said through the mind link.

While I didn't know if he could hear me, he didn't respond, which killed me more on the inside. I had to endure my wolf, her aggression, and that stupid brainwashing liquid that Thiago pumped into me all by myself.

It was so damn lonely. I had no control.

My wolf stabbed him in the underbelly with her extended claws. Pain ripped through my chest, my heart shattering into a million fucking pieces at the sudden hurt in his eyes. He stumbled back and squeezed his eyes closed for the briefest moment to heal his wound.

But it didn't seal right back up like it usually did. This wound was deep.

"Harder, Bria," Thiago called from the edge of the battlefield as he walked backward through the woods, probably to somewhere safer. "You've weakened him enough. I want you to kill him. Go for his stomach."

At the sound of Thiago's orders, my wolf went crazy. She stalked toward our mate like he was some kind of prey, licked her bloody lips, and roared at Callum, our fucking mythology professor, because Thiago told us to.

"Please," I cried to my wolf through our mind link. *"Please, stop this."*

"Kill," she growled back. *"Kill Callum."*

"He's our mate! Our mate!" I growled back, desperate to take control and not submit to her.

There wasn't a damn chance in hell that I could kill Callum, but my wolf didn't even recognize him as our mate anymore. She called him by his first name, which she never did.

She saw him as a threat. Not as the man we loved.

This wasn't right.

This wasn't fucking right.

"Stop!" I screamed at her. *"Now! Please!"*

I tried desperately to dig my heels into the ground, to heal, to stop, to do something.

But my wolf was stronger than my will. Fighting against a ruthless, savage beast wasn't an option. I didn't have any fight in me; I had been running and hiding from Thiago all my life. Now, I had a fucking wolf inside of me who wouldn't stop hurting the only person who ever loved her.

Seeing an opening, my wolf forced me to leap forward and pummel Callum onto his back so hard that I heard a crack in what must've been his spine. Terror rushed through me. I couldn't stop this, nor could I stop her.

We stalked toward him, our blood-soaked teeth bared at our mate.

With those golden eyes, Callum stared up at me. Not in fear. Not in fright. In anguish.

He wasn't going to fight me back. He wasn't going to stop me. He made that clear.

"Please," I begged her. *"Don't do this."*

My wolf stepped over him, one paw on either side of his body, then sank her canines into his underbelly. She sank her teeth as deeply as they could go and pulled back up with a chunk full of his flesh in her mouth.

I tasted Callum's blood, his flesh on my tongue.

Blood poured out of his wound, creating a puddle on the ground underneath him. I forced my wolf to drop his flesh from our mouth and backed up slowly, wanting her to see what she had done, the pain she had caused.

This was never supposed to happen.

Why couldn't she snap out of it?

"Bria," Callum said through the link, his voice soft, almost like a whisper. *"I love you."*

My entire body froze, hearing each word fade into oblivion, one softer than the next. He closed his eyes, and I feared that he would never open them up again. His muscles all relaxed, his clenched jaw relaxing.

This couldn't be how it ended.

Standing over his body, I shook my head.

"Mate," my wolf whispered to me, pain shooting through our entire body and finally realizing what we had done. *"We hurt mate."*

Chapter Fifty-Six

CALLUM

My own mate bit to kill me.

Unable to stop myself, I shifted into my human form and grasped my bleeding abdomen. Blood poured out of my stomach, the muscle torn in three different places. I winced and scrambled back, pain shooting through me and my wolf.

"Bria," I whispered, wanting her to gain back control.

She could do it. She could escape whatever type of spell that Thiago had placed over her. This wasn't the real her, and it surely wasn't her wolf. If her wolf recognized me, she wouldn't be reacting this way. We were mates, forged by the Moon Goddess.

"Bria, answer me," I whispered through the link, wanting her to acknowledge me. *"Mate."*

Instead of answering me or even looking me in the eyes, she backed up a couple of inches. Fear flashed through her eyes. As if she finally understood what she had done, Bria stopped and stared at me in complete shock. Then, she turned around in disgrace and sprinted after Thiago, following in his fucking footsteps while I bled out everywhere because of her.

She didn't answer me. She didn't look in my direction. She just took off through the woods, running after Thiago, who had brainwashed her into thinking that I needed to be eliminated, that I needed to die by her hands.

Thiago must've still had control of her.

In a wave, all of Thiago's warriors followed Bria through the woods, rushing past her and running faster and harder to follow Thiago to wherever he had gone. I stumbled to my feet and toward her, tripping over my own legs and collapsing to the ground.

"Mate hurt us," my wolf said through my head, his voice lower than it usually was.

He didn't understand that this wasn't Bria. All he thought was that the woman we waited over forty-three years for had intentionally bitten us because she wanted to kill us, that she didn't love us anymore and would do anything in her power to run away.

Determined to prove him wrong, I stood to my feet again, walked two feet, and fell. Blood poured between my fingers, and I called out for Bria to stop again. I called her name, first and then last, told her that her mate wanted her back, that we still loved her, no matter what.

Yet she didn't stop running.

She would go back to Thiago to regroup and come at us harder and faster than they had last time. Who knew what kind of torture shit he had been hiding around the castle? I had seen the stuff he had in the prison cells and dungeon.

If they captured my pack ...

I glanced around to see my pack and Adan's pack lying on the battlefield. Most were still alive, but some weren't moving even in the slightest. I clenched my jaw and growled again, standing and moving forward another few feet.

Someone needed to stop Thiago.

If I didn't stop it, Bria would kill me and have to live like that forever.

My mate deserved more than that. She barely knew about wolves, barely understood how we lived or how to control herself. Thiago knew exactly what he was doing this entire time. He was grooming her to be his perfect pet, to be the destruction of the wolf species.

If there was even a sliver of her conscience left, she must've been terrified.

I wouldn't let her do this by herself. I would fight like hell for her.

So, despite my bleeding stomach, I shifted into my wolf and followed behind her.

Chapter Fifty-Seven

BRIA

Callum followed me.

My wolf listened to his slower and unsteady footsteps behind me.

I pumped my legs faster and farther than I thought I could, than I ever had. I had never been a runner, but I refused to stop and refused to let Callum catch up to me. I feared that I would lose control again and kill him.

What was worse ... I didn't think that I could go back to face him.

My wolf fucking hurt him. *I allowed her* to bite him, to rip his flesh from his body, to almost kill him. How could I ever forgive myself for something as fucked up as that? How could I ever face Callum again?

Thiago made me into my worst nightmare.

Callum Lee, my professor and the strongest man I had met, wouldn't forgive me for this.

A mate who wanted to kill him and hurt his pack was not a great mate, not even a good one. I was nothing but a terrible piece of shit for what I had done to them all. I caused all of this. If I had gone to Thiago when he asked the first time, I would've never met them.

Once I had lost Callum—and I was fucking sure of it—I found my way back to Thiago, sniffing out his scent through the thick mud and wooded area around his pack. I had been here so many times; I knew where that asshole was hiding.

Like I expected, I found him surrounded by a group of at least a hundred warriors, his muscles taut and jaw clenched, eyes a golden fury. He had expected me to kill Callum, and maybe he thought I did because when he saw me, he smiled.

That psychopath smiled.

"You've done it, Bria," he said to me, crouching at my level, wiping the blood off my chin with his forefinger, and tasting it. "You're free of his chains. Callum will never once walk this earth again and challenge me. Everyone will yield to us, *to me*."

All I wanted to do was leap at him, to fucking kill him here.

But I feared that I wasn't strong enough. Thiago had always been stronger, faster, and smarter than me. He had captured me, convinced my parents to give me up for money, ran countless tests on me.

He knew every bit of me, better than I knew myself.

So, I stood by his side and tried to come up with something.

Not wanting him to realize that I had broken out of the chains he molded around my mind, I howled in response. I hoped to the Moon Goddess that he didn't see the tears in my eyes, that he didn't know by the way I cowered, that he couldn't feel the pain shooting through every fucking inch of my body.

I didn't deserve the title of mate.

My chest tightened. I stared at the ground, trying to figure out a way to get Thiago alone because I wouldn't—couldn't—defeat him like this, not with his entire pack gathered around and awaiting his every order.

There were far too many of them, and my heart was in far too much pain.

The anguish was bone fucking deep, a pain that hurt my entire soul.

"We're going to finish them off, to kill them all unless they surrender to me," Thiago announced to the warrior wolves, who stood in wolf form around me. "Kill every last one of them, except the women and the children. They will be useful in reproducing."

Like zombies, the wolves turned toward the direction of Callum's and Adan's packs.

Ready to kill.

I couldn't wait any longer, knowing that if Thiago and his wolves marched back on Callum and Adan and their packs, they would kill them all. I knew what I had to do. I knew that I had to kill Thiago right here and right now.

No matter if he controlled hundreds of wolves.

No matter if he turned them all on me.

No matter if he killed me.

After letting out a low and feral growl, I stopped in my tracks and refused to follow him.

Thiago stopped a moment later and tilted his head to the side, making a come-hither motion with his fingers. "Come here, pup."

For a moment, the urge to follow him shot through my body, urging me forward, to keep moving, to follow his every order and demand. But I pushed my paws into the dirt and fought the incredible force.

Thiago turned around, eyes flashing gold, and growled, "Come here now, Bria."

Still, I fought the force and didn't move.

The other warrior wolves that he controlled stopped moving forward toward where Callum's pack was located and turned to face me, some watching curiously and others readying to attack not Thiago, but *me*.

And I didn't doubt that they would.

"Don't make me tell you again, Bria," Thiago said. "Or there will be consequences."

I guessed that he didn't understand that consequences didn't matter to me anymore. I had just given up the best thing in my life, had nearly killed the man I loved more than anything, the man whose pup might be inside my belly right now.

Instead of following blindly, I growled, "No."

Thiago roared loudly, so loud that my fur blew back. "NOW!"

"No."

Thiago shifted into his wolf and growled to the others, *"Make her surrender!"*

And so, amid the other warrior wolves lunging at me and snapping their jaws at me, I sprinted toward a shifted Thiago and sank my teeth into his neck. Then, I did something that I never thought I would get to do. I ripped out his throat and killed the fucker.

Chapter Fifty-Eight

CALLUM

With my abdomen bleeding profusely, I hobbled after Bria to find her. But with every step I took, my heart broke just a little bit more.

Bria couldn't control herself. This was the first time that I saw her as a wolf, the first time she had shifted, and I hadn't been there to help her out of it. Instead, I fucking let The Council take her from me. I let them brainwash her.

I knew that she wouldn't be able to control herself when she turned for the first time. I should've fucking been here. I should've been the one leading her and protecting her. But I hadn't been strong enough, nor had I been smart enough either.

Yet I persevered and continued.

"We aren't strong enough," my wolf said.

He had always been the one to hype me up, to make me stronger. Now, he didn't think he was good enough to protect Bria because she was stronger than he was and because she was the One Alpha. We had seen it with our own eyes.

Even though I wanted to succumb to the pain and the thoughts, I refused.

All that mattered was that Bria was out there, brainwashed and terrified of Thiago. When I marked that pretty neck of hers—hell, when I saw her walk through that hallway on the first day of class—I vowed to protect her from all the bad things in this life.

She wouldn't slip through my fingers that easily.

BRIA

Every one of the teeth-baring wolves around me suddenly stopped lunging at me, the darkness fading from their eyes and their bodies slowly transforming back into their humans. I glanced at every one of them and inhaled sharply, my breath catching.

"We're free," one said, dropping to her knees and sobbing uncontrollably. "Finally free."

Their aggression suddenly turned to intense excitement, their angry expressions transforming into happiness. Each and every one of them transformed from their wolves to their humans and began hugging each other.

They were free.

And ... I was free too.

Butterflies fluttered in my stomach, and I giggled. I fucking giggled the pain away. This was over. All of this was over. I wouldn't have to worry about Thiago messing with my life anymore. We were all free.

One of the warriors approached me. "Thank you so much for saving us."

"We'll do anything for you," another said, falling in front of me and bowing his head.

Suddenly, the other wolves followed suit and bowed their heads to me. I stared at them through wide and surprised eyes, not sure what this meant, but wolves did that to Callum. Maybe it was a sign of respect.

"You don't need to do anything for me," I said.

"Please," a younger male wolf said. "You must want something."

I glanced around the wolves and frowned, not sure what to say. "All I want is for this to be over. I don't want anything from any of you. I want to be happy and to be able to raise my pup without the constant fear of Thiago looming over me."

"We will do anything to protect you and your pup," the first man said, grinning widely.

My heart raced as I looked at each of the warriors. "I also want to help the community. I don't want this to ever happen again. I don't want anyone to fear that they're going to be taken or brainwashed. It's unacceptable."

I thought back to my first day of classes. I had been so timid, too timid to even tell Jasmine to back off the guy I liked. But now, I felt like I was the most powerful woman alive, and all I wanted to do was to stand up for the weak and girls and boys like me—the people who had been taken advantage of by anyone, even their family.

"I want to keep The Council." I stood firm in my decision. "But I want it to do good."

"We can do good," an older woman said to me. "We can save this world."

My lips curled into a smile, and I nodded. "I would love that."

"Anything for the One Alpha."

And while they all cheered and smiled, celebrated that they were free and that we would change this world for good, all I could think about was Callum. What would he think of me? I had hurt him—had nearly killed him—and endangered his pack. I didn't even know if Thiago brought them those duffel bags filled to the brim with medication. Did they even get healed?

Worst of all, I couldn't stop thinking that Callum would reject me the next time I saw him.

It was stupid to believe those smutty werewolf books that I had devoured when Callum first caught my eye, but everything in them had been true so far. Sometimes, alphas rejected their mates if they weren't particularly obedient enough.

And I had done *everything* to disobey Callum.

I betrayed him. I ran from him. I nearly killed him.

"No," my wolf whimpered, not even wanting me to think such things.

"We hurt him and his pack," I said, chest tightening. *"I wouldn't blame him if he did."*

The crowd in front of me suddenly became silent. I glanced toward them once more to see their heads bowed, as if they were giving me permission to lead them on this new and exciting opportunity.

But I didn't know the first thing about wolves even though I was one.

"Lead us," one wolf said. "Please."

Nervously, I nodded. "Okay," I whispered, glancing around until my gaze finally lifted from the warriors and to the wolves behind them. And that was when I saw Callum watching me from a distance, his gold eyes on me and his lips curled into a smile.

Chapter Fifty-Nine

CALLUM

I heard every part of her conversation.

What she wanted The Council to become. How she wanted to protect the world from monsters like Thiago. Why she needed to be sure that nobody else faced the same horrors as she had.

Everything.

She stood in the middle of the warriors, who all had their heads bowed to my mate, as she spoke stronger than I had ever seen her. When she waltzed into my class, she had been shy and timid, but not anymore.

My mate was growing into a strong and independent woman who didn't take shit.

Moonlight glimmering off her hair, she turned and looked over at me. Fear flashed into her eyes, her cheeks paling. She stopped talking and stared at me for the longest time. I held my side and smiled at her, hoping that she'd calm down.

I could feel how anxious she was through the mate bond.

Suddenly, she hurried toward me and wrapped her arms around my waist, pulling me close and resting her head on my chest. "I'm so sorry for leaving you. I thought what I was doing was for the best. I didn't want anyone to get hurt."

After scooping her into my arms, I winced at the pain from my wound, then spun her around and around, my nose buried deep in her hair, breathing in her scent and relaxing with her body pressed against mine. I ignored my wolf thinking that we weren't enough for her.

Because maybe we weren't as strong as One Alpha, but that didn't mean we wouldn't try to be like *her* for as long as we could.

"It's okay, Bria," I whispered, kissing her forehead and placing her down. "I know you wanted to do what was right. Any good luna would sacrifice their life for the pack even though you will *never*"—I grasped her chin in my hand and forced her to look up at me—"do something like that again."

Bria's eyes wavered.

I kissed her on the mouth. "Because I love you."

"You still love me?" she whispered.

And it broke my fucking heart. I grasped the sides of her face and drew her closer to me, pressing my body against hers so she knew that the only man who would ever touch her again was me. After placing another kiss on her lips, I rested my forehead against hers.

"Of course I still fucking love you." I kissed her again. "You're my mate."

"But I nearly killed you ..." She glanced down at the large scar on my abdomen that would never heal fully, and then she brushed her fingers against it and shivered. "I did this to you. I hurt you and endangered everyone."

"You were brainwashed."

"But still ..." Guilt built in her eyes. "I did this."

I stayed quiet, not wanting to say something wrong and make her feel worse. I could deal with the scar and the pain, but I wouldn't be able to deal with never seeing Bria again, especially if Thiago still had her.

"How did you know that you had One Alpha?" I asked, curious.

"Those books that you gave me. I didn't know what it was before I started reading them, but I remembered that when my parents would bring me to see Thiago—and I would go in and out of consciousness—that they were mentioning One Alpha. I thought it was ... a gene or something. Not a real wolf, not this strength or this power."

She glanced around at the warriors in The Council. "They want me to lead them, but how will I be good enough? I don't know anything about werewolves. I don't know how to lead them or how to ... to do what alphas do."

My lips curled into a grin, butterflies in my stomach for her. "You'll figure it out."

Still, I could see the hesitation in her eyes, so I decided to lighten the mood and ask her a question that had been nagging me since I stopped at the edge of the woods and listened to her little speech to The Council.

"So, you're pregnant?" I asked softly.

Her cheeks paled. "You heard?"

I drew my hand over her stomach and kissed her on the lips again, resting my forehead against hers. "I heard everything."

She gnawed on the inside of her cheek. "I don't know for certain yet, but Thiago's doctor had found something on one of the many tests he ran on me while he had me captured. I wanted to die there, Callum. I thought I deserved it, but when I found out that I might have a pup inside of me ... I couldn't stand the thought of not fighting for my life. I fought so hard for us."

"Maybe a little *us*"—he curled his fingers against my belly—"will show up soon."

And maybe, after forty-three years of waiting, I would finally get the life that every wolf strived for. I had a mate and maybe a pup too. The Moon Goddess had granted almost all of my wishes.

Only time would tell.

My Werewolf Professor continues in the two-part epilogue.

Also By Emilia Rose

Paranormal Romance

Submitting to the Alpha

Come Here, Kitten

Alpha Maddox

The Twins

Four Masked Wolves

Monster Lover

Contemporary Romance

Stepbrother

Poison

The Bad Boy

Detention

Excite Me

Erotica

Climax: Erotic One-Shot Collection

Also By Emilia Rose

Scan the QR code with your phone to view all of Emilia's books!

My Werewolf Professor Graphic Novel

Start reading the My Werewolf Professor graphic novel here.

About the Author

Emilia Rose is a *USA Today* best-selling author of steamy romance. Highly inspired by her study abroad trip to Greece in 2019, Emilia loves to include Greek and Roman mythology in her writing.

She graduated from the University of Pittsburgh with a degree in psychology and a minor in creative writing in 2020 and now writes novels as her day job.

With over 18 million combined book views online and a growing presence on reading apps, she hopes to inspire other young novelists with her tales of growth and imagination, so they go on to write the stories that need to be told.

Join Emilia's newsletter for exclusive giveaways, early chapter releases, and more!

www.ingramcontent.com/pod-product-compliance
Lightning Source LLC
Chambersburg PA
CBHW020331030826
48979CB00021B/606
9781954597808